PRISONER FROM PENANG

CLARE FLYNN

CRANBROOK PRESS

This book is dedicated to the memory of all those women and children who were incarcerated in Japanese internment camps between 1942 and 1945. Their courage and endurance in the face of years of extreme suffering is insufficiently acknowledged.

Prisoner from Penang © copyright 2020 Clare Flynn

Cranbrook Press

London, UK

ISBN 978-1-9164692-3-5

Cover design JD Smith Design

"We have had a great deal of bad news lately from the Far East, and I think it highly probable, for reasons which I shall presently explain, that we shall have a great deal more. Wrapped up in this bad news will be many tales of blunders and shortcomings, both in foresight and action. No one will pretend for a moment that disasters like these occur without there having been faults and shortcomings. I see all this rolling towards us like the waves in a storm..."

Winston Churchill, Address to the British Parliament, 27th January, 1942

PROLOGUE

George Town, Penang, December, 1945

She's gone. I think I made her uncomfortable. The sight of me. My refusal to talk about what happened to me during the occupation. Evie's my best friend – now my only friend – and I've just pushed her away.

I know I ought to feel bad about it, but I don't. I merely feel numb. Seeing her with her glossy hair and strong nails, her firm tanned skin, healthy from the Australian sunshine and daily swimming, made me want to shrink away and hide.

I'm a wrinkled, half-dead crone, a bag of bones, broken, soiled, damaged by what I've seen and what I had to do. And I'm only a few years older than she is – I'll be thirty-five next birthday and already an old woman. That's what war does to you.

No. That's what the Japanese have done to me.

When we were freed from the last internment camp, one of the doctors said that talking about what we'd been through would help us eventually come to terms with it. He was a big jolly Australian and kept spouting platitudes about troubles shared being troubles halved. All very well for him with his well-fed body, fresh out of medical school. His idea of trouble was probably waking up with a hangover when he had to sit an exam, or a dingo getting in among his daddy's sheep. What could he possibly know about what we were going through? He was in the business of saving lives, not seeing them end prematurely, brutally, savagely.

None of us voiced disagreement with that young doctor though. We just stared at him blankly, as if he were speaking a foreign language. We didn't even look at each other. We didn't need to. We were all thinking the same thing – that we would never, *ever* speak about that place and what had happened to us there.

So, even though she is my dearest friend, I will never tell Evie about it. How could she possibly understand? How could she recognise her friend, her daughter's teacher, in the creature I have become?

No. My memories are mine alone.

Yet maybe that Australian doctor had a point. I might not be able to tell anyone else, but perhaps one day, I could write it down. I can push it out of my brain and onto paper, then lock it away where it won't be found – or burn it – and try to get on with the rest of my life. My ruined, broken life.

PART I

MARY'S MEMOIR

1

SINGAPORE

our years earlier, December 1941

Singapore was utter chaos the morning we arrived. The island was already bursting with people retreating from the steady advance of the imperial Japanese army down the Malayan peninsula. Refugees like us, who still believed the promises from the authorities that the island of Singapore was impregnable.

But it was not only the civilian refugees who were deluded. The military and the powers-that-be all persisted in that delusion – even though the mounting evidence was to the contrary.

There were uniforms everywhere – men convinced they would succeed in defending the place that was the symbol of British imperial power. They were ready to send the Japs off with bloody noses. That was the way they talked – all bluff, bluster and bravado, like schoolboys getting ready for a conker fight.

But those of us who had fled through the night, crammed into train carriages escaping from Penang, knew differently. We had witnessed the bombs falling and the buildings burning and the complete annihilation of the British and Australian air force there. We women were impotent participants in the shameful abandonment of our island home as we were herded onto the ferries and trains to escape. So much for the supposedly indomitable white population – we were all scuttling away, abandoning our Malay and Chinese friends, our colleagues and servants, to their fate. And the Japs knew differently too. After they had taken possession of our beautiful island, hoisting their flag to replace the white one, which the locals had no choice but to fly after we'd run away, we heard their taunting radio broadcast. 'Hello, Singapore, this is Penang calling. Do you like our bombing?' That was when I knew nowhere was safe. Not even Fortress Singapore.

That December morning, Mum and I, along with the other women without children, were ordered to leave the train as soon as we reached Singapore. Those with children, including my friend, Evie Barrington, with her two, were told to remain on board, ready to be evacuated by ship immediately. Most of those mothers had been separated from their husbands when we got on the train, expecting to meet them again in Singapore in a couple of days. As soon as they found out they'd be going straight to board a ship, some of them started wailing and crying while others gave vent to anger. Not Evie. Her husband was already dead, months earlier. Not from bombs or battles, but from blood poisoning after a fall down a disused mine shaft in the jungle.

Funny isn't it, that both Evie and I had lost the men we loved before the war in Malaya had really got going. I'd lost two. Though my fiancé, Frank's death was still uncon-firmed, I'd stood and watched the Japs shoot down our RAF boys over the strait. I'd seen the airplanes explode in the sky, or catch fire, rolling into a spin and plummeting into the sea. I probably even saw Frank die. He'd warned me death was a strong possibility. The old Brewster Buffalos were ancient, underpowered and inadequate – no match for the Japanese with their faster, fleeter Mitsubishi fighter planes.

Frank and I had become engaged to marry just days before the bombing of Penang. He gave me the ring over a romantic dinner at the Runnymede. As the train moved through the dark Malayan night, I twisted that ring round and round on my finger, cursing God for once again dangling happiness in front of me, only to snatch it away as soon as my hands had closed around it.

Frank had known he was risking his life every time he climbed into the cockpit, every time the order to scramble came. But I didn't. I believed lightning never struck twice in the same place. I'd already had one fiancé die on me, so this time – surely – my happiness was going to last. Life couldn't be that cruel, could it? The man I'd been engaged to before, Ralph, had taken his own life after betraying me with a married woman who cast him off as soon as he'd dumped me. But I was soon to discover a depth of cruelty so extreme that back then I'd never have believed it.

That morning when I arrived in Singapore, I thought death had singled me out by taking both the men I'd wanted to marry. Now, I know better. Death doesn't discriminate. It takes its victims whenever a chance arises. And war gives death so many chances. A veritable feast of opportunities to harvest people and to do so in cruel and unendingly creative ways.

～

THE VOICE WAS ALL-TOO familiar and not one I wanted to hear.

'Coo-ee! Mary, Mary Helston! Wait!'

Veronica Leighton pushed her way through the crowd of confused women and children pouring out of the station in Singapore.

Of all the people on the planet, Veronica was the only person I truly loathed. She was the meanest, most gratuitously spiteful, nastiest woman I had ever met. When she'd left Penang to move to Singapore with her civil-servant husband about a year earlier, I'd rejoiced to see the back of her. It was she who had caused Ralph's suicide, and she'd also tried to make a play for Frank. And she'd done her best to make my friend Evie's life a misery from the moment Evie landed in Penang.

I thought Veronica hated me too. Yet here she was, battling through the crowd towards me with a friendly smile on her face.

She took hold of my arm, steering me away from the throng. 'Don't go with everyone else. You don't want to sleep on a camp-bed in a barrack room with a leaky roof. I have a nice hotel room lined up for you.'

Jerking my elbow from Veronica's grip, I put my arm around Mum and started to move back towards the flood of other women. 'Leave us be,' I said.

'Don't be silly, Mary. I moved heaven and earth to get that room for you.'

Seeing the look of scorn and disbelief on my face, she quickly added, 'Well, I got it for Evie and her brats actually, but she wasn't allowed off the train. I promised her to look out for you and your mother. She specifically asked me to make sure you got the room.'

I started to protest but seeing the exhaustion in my

mother's face and the long snake of women climbing into the back of army trucks, I hesitated, and Veronica pounced.

'You've absolutely no idea what it took me to get that room. The favours I had to call in.' She gave that little tinkling laugh of hers that had always irritated me so much. 'Take it or leave it, Mary. No skin off my nose.' She shrugged. 'I'm sure there are plenty of others who'll jump at it.'

Mum's face was telegraphing a silent plea to me. With Dad somewhere on the road between here and Penang, she was feeling lost and overwhelmed and depended on me. I swallowed my pride and accepted the offer.

THE HOTEL WASN'T GRAND, but it was clean and comfortable. After allowing us the rest of that day and night to settle in and recover from our journey and our hasty departure from Penang, Veronica arrived the following morning and asked if we would join her as volunteers at the military hospital.

Mum looked alarmed. She was worried sick that Dad had not yet managed to join us, and she didn't want to commit to doing anything until she had news of him. I think the idea of being surrounded by wounded and dying men frightened her too – little did she know that she would soon become accustomed to the sight of extreme suffering and death.

'Mum is completely banjaxed,' I said to Veronica. 'I'll come but she needs to rest.'

A pair of finely shaped eyebrows were raised at me in reply.

On the way to the hospital – Veronica brought me there in the front of the ambulance she was driving– she asked if I'd had news of Frank.

I hadn't even been aware that she knew his name. But I remembered she had tried to flirt with him at the Penang Club, and Veronica always made it her business to find out about everyone and everything.

'No. I've had no news, but I fear the worst.'

'Really?' She looked surprised. 'Shouldn't you be looking on the bright side? Mustn't be defeatist, darling.'

Her chirpy tone irritated me and I snapped at her, 'If you'd seen the smoke over Butterworth aerodrome when the Japanese blew up our planes you wouldn't say that.' I bit my lip. I could have added that I had watched as the few RAF planes that did manage to scramble were shot down over the strait like fish in a barrel, but I chose not to mention that. I didn't want to risk crying in front of Veronica.

And yet, even though I knew instinctively that Frank was dead, I couldn't help but harbour the hope that he might appear among the wounded, so being at the hospital felt right. To acknowledge that he was gone forever was too painful. In the meantime, I would try to take some comfort in helping care for other poor wounded men, whose wives or girlfriends were far away.

'I'll find out for you. I know everyone who's anyone, including Brooke-Popham,' she said, referring to the Commander in Chief of the British Far East Command. Veronica had never been slow to drop names. 'If your chap's dead, it's better that you know, so you can get on with the rest of your life.' She gave a dry laugh. 'Although what kind of life is that going to be? The idiots in power are still making out that we're safe as houses here.'

I wanted to scream. She was the most insensitive woman I had ever met.

THE ALEXANDRA BRITISH MILITARY HOSPITAL was about four miles to the west of the city. The pride of Singapore, the newly constructed hospital was said to be the best military medical facility in the world and had opened only about six months earlier. Staffed by Queen Alexandra nurses shipped in from Britain and Australia, the mass influx of wounded men meant they now needed to be supplemented by volunteer civilian nurses. The hospital, which boasted all the latest modern equipment, including x-ray machinery and air-conditioned operating theatres, was able to accommodate over three hundred patients.

As I approached the entrance to report for duty, I was nervous. Being medically untrained, I felt an imposter entering the building, a three-storey, white stucco, colonial style building, surrounded by lawns and trees.

I was asked to report to an office on the ground floor, where a harassed middle-aged civilian woman ticked my name off a list and told me to go up to a ward on the first floor and ask for Sister Brewster.

The nursing sister was dressed in a crisp white uniform with matching starched veil. She looked me up and down and gave her head a shake, evidently asking herself why she was having to deal with an unqualified minion.

'I don't know why they keep sending us VADs. It's trained nurses we need. Just make sure you don't get in the way.'

'I'll do my best. What would you like me to do?'

I expected to be given auxiliary nursing duties – washing out bedpans and sick bowls and changing beds. As a schoolteacher, I was long past the point of being squeamish. I'd had to clean up after many small children when they were sick or had accidents – often the kind that required clean underwear.

'The boys in here are badly injured. Some of them need help with writing letters home. Think you can manage that?'

'Of course. I'm a teacher.' I tried not to sound as affronted as I felt.

She cracked a smile. 'I didn't mean it in that way. It's just that some of the chaps are in a pretty bad state. Don't want you blubbing over them or fainting on me.' Seeing my expression, she added. 'You think I'm joking! The last VAD we had up here only lasted two hours.'

'I think I can manage better than that.'

All the beds in the ward were occupied. I'd no idea so many soldiers had already been injured, nor the scale of their injuries. I swallowed. I was nervous as I approached the bed to meet my first patient.

At first, I thought he was asleep. I was about to move on to the next name on my list. But something made me linger a moment. I picked up the chart hanging on the end of the bed and read that he was Australian, twenty-two-years-old, a victim of shrapnel wounds from shellfire, now recovering from an operation to remove his right arm.

As I put the clipboard back, I saw he was awake. He'd just had his eyes closed.

'G'day,' he said cheerily, immediately putting me at ease. 'You're a new girl, aren't you? Where you from?'

He was a good-looking chap with light brown curly hair, blue eyes and a friendly smile. His accent left no doubt as to his national origins.

'Penang. I arrived here yesterday.'

'Hear you had it bad up there. The Nips have been giving it quite a hammering. What's your name, Sheila?'

'It's certainly not Sheila.' I couldn't help smiling. 'It's

Mary.' I glanced up at the sign above his bed. 'Nice to meet you, Corporal Murphy.'

'Call me Charlie. We Aussies don't stand on ceremony.'

'Righty-ho, Charlie it is. Now, we'd better get on with it. I've quite a few lads to see today.' I pulled up a chair at his bedside. 'Who are we writing to?'

'Mum and Dad.' He told me their address and I wrote it down, waiting for him to start dictating. He thought for a moment, before saying, 'Dear Mum and Dad, sorry it's taken me a while to get round to writing to you, only I've been so busy having a good time I never seemed to find the right moment to pick up a pen, but at least I'm doing it now. Don't be worrying about me as I'm having a ball here. Not seen any action, just a bit of trench digging and bashing the parade ground. I've been doing a lot of swimming and going to parties. Singapore is a bonza place.'

I had been struggling to keep up, but I stopped and stared at him.

He shrugged, then tapped his nose. 'Don't want the old dears worrying unduly.'

My mouth gaped wide. 'You're not going to tell them about your arm?'

'They'll find out soon enough. A one-armed soldier is good for no one. Army'll be sending me back Down Under as soon as there's space on a ship. Women and children first.'

'But surely your parents must know what's happening here? They'll have seen the news reels.'

He snorted. 'No, mate, they live out in the bush. They get their news when they leave the station and go into town for supplies. And before you ask, that's only every few months. We're fifty miles from the nearest town.' He grinned. 'I could well see them before this letter gets there. But just in case I don't, there's no need to give the old girl sleepless nights worrying about me. And Dad'll take it bad too. You can't work a sheep station with a missing arm.'

There was no trace of self-pity about that young man. His future had been ruined by a mortar bomb and yet he was determined to remain cheerful – or at least to present a cheerful face to the outside world.

'What will you do, when you get back to Australia, if you can't work with sheep?'

'God knows. I'll worry about that when the time comes. Maybe I'll find a girl who isn't too picky, and we can open a bar somewhere. I'll count the money and she can serve the beers.' He grinned and gave me a wink. 'What about you, Miss Mary? Looks like you've got yourself a fella.' He nodded at my engagement ring.

'Missing in action. RAF. Shot down over Penang.'

I swallowed down the tears. I hadn't allowed myself to cry for Frank yet, believing that if I did, it would be admitting there was no hope.

'Sorry, Mary. That's rough. Those RAF and RAAF boys were incredibly brave, flying planes that were only fit for the scrapheap. You should be very proud of your fiancé.'

I swallowed again. 'As your parents will be of you.'

'Maybe. But I doubt it. They didn't want me to join up. But no one's going to call me a coward or a bludger. No chance. With a bit of luck, I'll get out alive. Not in one piece, but alive'll do. I lost some good mates in the fighting here. I've had enough.'

Charlie gasped and squeezed his eyes tightly shut.

'Can I get you something? Shall I call a nurse?'

He shook his head and forced a smile. 'It's the arm. It hurts like hell. As if it was still there. Terrible pain in my fingers. Only I haven't got any fingers.' He grinned at me, but I could tell he was suffering. 'Don't worry, Mary. It'll pass.'

'Shall we leave the letter until another time? I can come back after I've done the other chaps.'

'No. We're done. That's all I want to say.'

I turned to go, then something struck me. 'Won't your parents wonder why the letter isn't in your handwriting? Won't they guess something's wrong?'

He gave a chuckle. 'I doubt they've ever seen my handwriting. Not a lot of call for it when you're rounding up sheep all day.'

THAT EVENING when I got back to the hotel, I found Veronica Leighton waiting for me in the lobby. She was sipping a gin sling and idly flipping through the pages of a magazine. My heart lurched. She must have heard news.

Veronica looked up and saw me, throwing the magazine aside and patting the sofa beside her. 'How did you get on at the hospital?' she asked.

'Fine,' I said, not wanting to engage in small talk with a woman I still loathed. Then, relenting – she had after all found me a hotel room and work – I added, 'All they had me do was write letters home for servicemen who are unable to write themselves. Not as important as driving an ambulance I suppose, or nursing those poor chaps.'

Veronica ignored the intended barb and said, 'An ambulance is no more difficult to drive than a car.' Her lips tightened. 'I have bad news for you I'm afraid, Mary.'

I nodded, knowing what was coming and willing myself not to break down in front of Veronica. If I'd managed to control my tears until now, I could manage a little longer.

'Flight Lieutenant Francis James Hyde-Underwood was shot down over the Strait of Malacca on the morning of December the 9th. I understand they got his fuel tanks and the plane exploded. He would have died instantly. I'm frightfully sorry, darling.' She touched my arm with her hand, but I brushed it away.

'Thank you. I appreciate you finding out for me. I knew he was dead, but I had to be sure.' I got up.

'Those boys were incredibly brave, but they never stood a chance. The airfield at Butterworth was completely wiped out. And we all know those aeroplanes hadn't a hope against the Japanese ones. Too slow to climb. No speed to get out of trouble. It's a bloody disgrace. Apparently, there are some Hurricanes on the way. Too bloody late now. If it's any consolation, my contact told me your chap gave it all he had. Seems to have been a popular fellow.'

I didn't want to listen to Veronica's eulogy for the man I loved. Not after the way she'd tried to flirt with him under my nose. I was glad she'd taken the trouble to find out for me, but it wouldn't stop me hating her with a passion that surprised even myself.

'Any news of your father?' she asked, giving the impression she was actually interested but, knowing Veronica, it was more likely that she wanted to move away from the topic of Frank.

'No. And I've no idea how he's going to find us. He's driving down in Reggie Hyde-Underwood's car but there's been no word. I imagine the roads are frightfully clogged up.'

'The most likely place to find out is Robinson's. Everyone's going there to find each other. If he's not there it'll be Raffles or the Swimming Club.'

Veronica was referring to Singapore's department store,

Robinson's, whose restaurant and tearoom had always been a must on the itinerary of any visitor to the city. The place had taken a hit from a Japanese bomb less than two weeks earlier on December 8th but, according to Veronica, had opened its doors for business as usual the following day.

'Your best bet,' she said, cheerily, 'is to let the manager in each of those places know where you're staying, but I'd also stop by Robinson's in person every day to make sure.'

'I can't understand why he isn't here yet.' I was dreading telling Mum that there was still no word.

Veronica waved a hand airily. 'I suppose it depends on whether they have to keep taking cover to avoid Japanese bombers. Not to mention roadblocks and traffic. Don't forget the army will be clogging up the roads too. I don't think you can expect to see him for several days.'

She got up, straightened her skirt and gave me a bright smile. 'Chin up, Mary.'

Then she was gone, her signature Shalimar scent lingering behind her.

Free at last to cry about losing Frank, I couldn't do it. I didn't even shed any tears when I got to the bedroom. I didn't want to do that in front of Mum when her own nerves were so fragile. Telling her that Dad might not be here for a while brought on another weeping fit from her. It was up to me to keep calm and stay strong. I needed to be cheerful and try to sustain her spirits.

But later, once Mum was asleep, I lay in the blackout-darkened bedroom and prayed that Frank's death hadn't been prolonged or painful. I thought of him, trapped in a burning cockpit, plunging through thick smoke towards the sea. How long would it have taken for him to die? Would he have known he'd 'copped it' as he used to say? That he was 'gone for a Burton' – the odd English expression he and the other pilots used so often when a colleague was shot down?

People say your whole life flashes before your eyes in the moment of dying. I was such a tiny portion of Frank's life, timewise, yet I hope a very large part in importance to him. He had been everything to me, so I hope it had been true for him too.

That night, I finally wept silent tears until the pillow was soaked under my head and, all cried out, I fell into a dreamless sleep.

DAD HAD STILL NOT ARRIVED by Christmas. It was a miserable affair that year. On Christmas Day, Hong Kong surrendered, a terrible humiliation for the British Empire in the east. The Japanese were pushing the Allied forces further down the Malay peninsula to Singapore. What had once been a bastion, an impregnable fortress, the symbol of British power, was another fragile skittle waiting to fall.

The disastrous collapse of Hong Kong was a shock to the residents of Singapore. The British there, and until recently further up the peninsula, had largely ignored the war and refused to recognise the Japanese threat.

British women in particular had been living in ignorance and continuing with their pampered expatriate way of life – enjoying the sunshine, the parties, the leisure pursuits and servants to do virtually everything from childcare to catering. And among the men there was a conspiracy of self-delusion. It was simply unthinkable to imagine the British and our mighty empire falling prey to the inferior numbers of the invading Japanese.

I'm certain this inbuilt prejudice and innate arrogance

explains why the military leadership was so hesitant in acting promptly and decisively to cut short the Japanese advance, even though the Allies significantly outnumbered the enemy. There was also a lack of preparation – in part due to bad planning and in part to the lack of the necessary aircraft and anti-tank guns. Underpinning all this was a deeply-rooted belief among the British that the Japanese were inferior. But to me, at the time, it was just one great big enormous mess.

As I was to discover as the war proceeded, that ingrained belief about the racial superiority of white men in general and the British in particular, was all too evident to the Japanese and may well account for the enthusiasm with which they perpetrated their atrocities. Bringing the proud British low, treating them with the height of cruelty and depravity, was a way of drumming home that the status quo had well and truly changed.

IN EARLY JANUARY, Dad finally turned up. Reggie Hyde-Underwood's motorcar had got a flat tyre, which caused a significant delay, as the spare was missing, probably stolen. It struck me as deeply ironic that their progress was halted for the absence of a rubber tyre, when Reggie was a rubber planter and all around were acres of rubber trees and abandoned latex processing factories.

As Veronica had predicted, Reggie had discovered our whereabouts via Robinson's and dropped Dad off at our hotel.

Until I saw my father standing there in the hotel lobby in front of me, I hadn't realised how worried I'd been about his absence. I'd been so busy putting a brave face on for

Mum that I hadn't allowed my own concerns for him to surface. I flung my arms around him and hugged him tight in relief.

Behind Dad, I saw Reggie was waiting. I thanked him for bringing my father safely to Singapore and remembered I needed to tell him about the confirmation of his brother's death. After Dad went up to the room to find Mum, I broke the news.

Reggie closed his eyes for a moment, and his mouth set hard as he tried to control his emotions. 'I knew there was practically no chance that he'd survived, but I kept on hoping.'

'Me too,' I said.

Reggie leant towards me and gave my hand a squeeze.

'I couldn't help thinking that maybe he'd managed to bail out and been picked up by a boat.' He noticed the ring on my left hand. 'So, he asked you to marry him?'

I nodded, tears welling in my throat. 'Two days before he was killed. The last time I saw him.'

'I'm so terribly sorry, Mary. What a bloody mess.' He looked down, his eyes fixed on his knees. 'I've just heard my wife and son have already left Singapore.' He looked glum. 'Not even a chance to say goodbye.'

'You'll go after them though? To Australia?'

'As soon as I can. But men are expected to stay for the foreseeable. Do the right thing. See off the Yellow Peril. Anyway, I've things to sort out here first. Banking arrangements for Susan in Australia. That kind of thing. And I'll have to wait until I hear from her as to where exactly she is. No one here seems to have a bloody clue what's happening. Meanwhile, I'm going to do what I can for civil defence.'

He studied my face. 'Get yourself and your parents out of here, Mary. As soon as you can. I don't have a good feeling about our ability to hold out. And not a lot of confidence in the idiots making all the decisions.'

I didn't tell him that, without Frank, I no longer cared whether I lived or died. Instead, I muttered that we would leave as soon as I could manage it but meanwhile, I was making myself useful as a VAD.

Reggie was a big bulk of a man, like an unkempt bear, so very different from Frank that no one would ever have imagined them to be brothers. Yet there was something about his manner, the timbre of his voice and the kindness in his eyes that made my tears well up again.

There was an awkward silence. We had nothing left to say to each other. I made my excuses and went back up to the hotel room to join my parents.

2

FLIGHT FROM SINGAPORE

L ike most of the civilian men, Dad was expected to get involved with the civil defence efforts. Together with Reggie Hyde-Underwood and many others we had known in Penang: officials, professionals, planters and businessmen – Dad was sent to dig ditches and fortifications on the northern shore of the island.

When he came back to the hotel after his first stint, I could see he was finding it hard. I glanced at Mum and could tell she saw it too. Dad looked haggard, older than his years, and the dark rings under his eyes indicated his exhaustion. Not a tall man, he appeared visibly shrunken since we'd left Penang.

'Why are you having to dig trenches? I thought they'd been building up the defences for months if not years.' Mum sounded irritable.

Dad sighed. 'They built them all facing the sea. They reckoned that was the only way the Japs would attack.'

Mum clasped her throat. 'I don't understand. They've been saying for ages that Singapore is safe. Why the sudden panic? If the Japs are going to attack by land why didn't we think of that?'

'I suppose because everyone thought it was impossible,' I said.

Dad had experienced first-hand the flight of our troops back down the peninsula. 'No one dreamt they'd dare to do what they've done – land in the north and travel south on fleets of bicycles.'

'And we can't stop a bunch of bicycles?' Mum was incredulous.

'Not when they have squadrons of aircraft bombing the path in front of them.'

FOUR DAYS AFTER CHRISTMAS, nightly bombing began and continued every night for a week. Mum's frayed nerves were at breaking point and it was only the relief of having Dad with us that kept her going. I was glad my hospital duties took me away from her. I tried to persuade her to volunteer herself, but she'd agree then kept putting it off. I suspect she didn't want to have to face how bad the situation was in the hospital, where every day more wounded men arrived for treatment.

In our hotel, the walls shook, our beds rocked, the glass in the window juddered. My fear was in contrast to the reassuring bluster of most of my compatriots.

During January, more and more people flooded onto the island from the peninsula, and military reinforcements arrived by sea.

Too little too late.

The ships that brought them through the heavily mined

harbour, unloaded, then departed again, bearing women and children. Although, even by mid-January, there were relatively few takers and many ships left half empty. Looking back, I can see this was a contributing factor to the subsequent tragedies that could have been avoided with less braggadocio and more caution.

Dad constantly nagged Mum and me to get out of Singapore, but my mother wouldn't contemplate being parted from Dad and by then I was so absorbed in the work I was doing, that I would have felt guilty abandoning my job as a VAD.

I'd met so many young men, mostly British, but also Australians. Most, like Charlie, were stoical about their suffering but there were one or two who cried when they thought no one could see them, their lives changed irrevocably by their injuries and their experience of battle. Home must have seemed impossibly far away. For me to abandon them would have felt cowardly and cruel.

And to be honest, I didn't relish the idea of leaving Singapore or Malaya. My home since childhood had been Penang. England held no appeal for me. Why leave one battle scene to walk right into another?

Most of those who did leave headed to Australia – it was close and, so far, safe. But, to be honest, our decision to remain was typical of the majority of women in the colony – even many of those with children. The idea of leaving never entered our heads. How could we possibly scuttle away and leave the men behind?

Most *mems* had built their adult lives here in the Straits Settlements, and the concept of the life we had always known collapsing was simply unthinkable. We were doughty women of the British Empire and we intended to stand our ground.

THE NURSES I worked among were heroines. They were a mixture of Queen Alexandra nurses – the QAs, Australian military nurses, and civilian nurses. Some were long-time Singaporeans and others recent volunteers – but all were models of courage and professionalism. I met one or two who had chosen to come east soon after the war began, fleeing the bombs and rationing back in Britain for an adventure in an exciting and exotic location. They had little dreamt that the war would catch them up out here, but I never saw a single one of them flinch from the challenge.

As for Veronica, I went out of my way to avoid her. That wasn't hard. Although we were both working as VADs, our paths rarely crossed. We did come near one afternoon when I was hurrying down a corridor in the hospital and saw her talking to one of the porters. As always, she appeared to be flirting with the man – a Eurasian who can't have been more than twenty. Just in time I ducked behind a pillar then reversed my steps and took the long way round to where I was headed.

AS THE JAPANESE moved inexorably towards us down the long thin peninsula, morale in the colony began to dip. At last, people began to acknowledge that we British were not invincible after all.

On 11th February 1942, at the hospital, the Principal Matron addressed all the nursing staff and the volunteers. Reputed to be a stern but kind woman, I had never had any involvement with her. She stood on a stool and spoke in a firm and businesslike manner.

'I have received orders from the highest authority that all nursing staff must leave the colony immediately.'

There was a collective gasp.

'A small skeleton staff will be remaining. I am not asking for volunteers, as I know you would all step forward. Those of you who will be remaining already know who you are. The rest of you should proceed immediately to the harbour, where ships will be waiting to transport you to safety. May God bless you all and I thank you for your tireless service.'

She clambered down from her stool, leaving us with more questions than answers. I was standing close to her and saw the unshed tears glistening in her eyes. The nursing staff was already overstretched. How on earth would a skeleton staff cope? It appeared that the authorities were at the point of capitulating and abandoning the precious jewel that was Singapore to the mercy of the invading army.

There were so many patients, and the bombing so bad, that new admissions were lying on the floor awaiting treatment in the absence of sufficient beds. As we moved between them, heading for the exit, the floor was sticky with blood.

For the past several days my role as letter scribe had been abandoned in favour of assisting the nursing staff. Untrained, I had been put to work preparing and applying bandages and dressings, washing wounds, sluicing bedpans and fetching and carrying. I held the hands of dying men, bearing witness to their passing.

As we followed the orders to leave, the eyes of those exhausted wounded men looked up at us as we said our goodbyes. It was as if they were saying 'That's it. It's all up for us. We've had it.'

My first patient, Charlie, had been discharged a few days

earlier. Although I was sure a missing arm was insufficient to justify a priority place on a ship, I prayed he'd make it out of Singapore before it was too late.

As we left the hospital, we could hear rifle fire from just a couple of miles away. The air was thick with smoke and the smell of explosives. The city of Singapore, the British Empire's pride and joy was descending rapidly into chaos. As I hurried back to the hotel on foot, the skies were lit up with the streaks of tracer fire, and the sound of exploding mortars followed our progress.

I walked with a group of doctors and nurses. We barely spoke. All of us were experiencing a sense of abandonment and betrayal by our government and military. None of us wanted to leave our patients. I was not the only one anxious about their fate and that of the few doctors and nurses who were remaining to care for them.

The road into the city was constantly strafed by Japanese aircraft, machine-gunning anyone visible, without mercy. A couple of times the only place where we were able to take cover was in an open ditch by the side of the road. Believe me, when your life is at stake, you'll do anything to stay alive, even when that ditch is an open sewer.

When, at last, I walked into the hotel bedroom I was sharing with my parents, Mum looked at me in horror.

'Mary! What in heaven's name has happened to you? You're filthy.' She clamped a hand over her mouth.

I tried to make light of it. 'I managed to fall into a drainage ditch. I had to walk back from the hospital.' I started to pull off my clothes. I wouldn't be wearing them again. There was no time for laundry.

The situation since the bombing of Penang had disturbed Mum's equilibrium. She constantly worried about

Dad, who was finding the heavy physical work tough. Recently retired from an office job, being plunged into doing vigorous labouring must have been an ordeal. Yet he never complained. It was Mum who struggled. She couldn't accept what had happened to us. She wanted to wake up, find herself back in Penang, going to her weekly bridge games, knitting socks for soldiers in Europe, baking cakes and doing her daily crossword puzzle. It was impossible for her to believe that the war had come to us.

After I had quickly washed and changed my clothes, I saw Mum was crying. Back in Penang, she had always been the most cheerful of people, content with life, retaining a robust sense of humour. Now she was crumbling in front of me.

Bombs were dropping in the nearby docks, obliterating the godowns and destroying the food and raw materials stored in them. As we talked, the walls of the hotel shook.

'We have to leave, Mum. We have to get down to the harbour and onto a ship. If we don't go, right away, there might not be any room left.' I waved the piece of paper I had been issued with that morning. 'I think we're on the point of surrendering.' I bit my lip as soon as the words were out. It felt awful to be verbally acknowledging the inevitable.

'I'm not budging without your father.' Her face was a mixture of defiance and terror.

'Mum, we have to go.' I started throwing clothing into a couple of holdalls. 'Otherwise we'll be blown up or the Japanese will capture us. They're only a couple of miles up the road from the hospital.' I put an arm around her shoulder. 'It's over, Mum. It's just a matter of time until they reach us here. We *have* to get out.' I tried to keep my voice calm, but I wanted to grab her and shake her.

Mum stared at me. 'I'm not moving. There's nowhere to

go. I'd rather stay here and die with your father. You can go, but don't expect me to come with you, Mary.'

Before I could reply, there was a hammering on the bedroom door. I opened it and Veronica Leighton was standing there. Her face was filthy, streaked with dirt, and her white shirt was splashed with blood. She pushed past me into the room.

'We have to go. NOW! There are a few ships in port, and they'll be sailing at dawn, and we need to be on one if we're going to get out of here alive.'

Mum's head was bent low and she didn't even acknowledge Veronica's presence.

'Come along, Mrs Helston. Pip pip!' Veronica clapped her hands. 'Only one small bag with the essentials. The ship will be extremely crowded.'

Mum didn't move.

'She refuses to go without Dad.'

'She'll have to.' Veronica moved to the bed and grabbed my mother's elbow. If it weren't for the gravity of the situation, I'd have been amused at the picture of the petite and elfin Veronica struggling to pull my overweight mum up and onto her feet.

Mum jerked her arm free and snarled at Veronica. 'I've told you. I'm not going.'

A deafening crash shook the room and a yawning space appeared where the window had been. Smoke and dust billowed inside between the shredded remains of the curtains. Veronica and I were coughing but my mother was screaming.

Veronica turned to me, and through her splutters managed to ask, 'Are you just going to let her die? Come on. We'll grab an arm each.'

We took Mum by the arms. She was wailing, sobbing

and trailing her feet on the floor, as she tried to resist us. Somehow, we managed to manoeuvre her down the staircase and into the foyer of the hotel where people were rushing about in aimless panic. Acrid smoke was everywhere, although the structure of this part of the hotel appeared undamaged. Through the clouds of dust, I saw my father coming towards us and I heaved an enormous sigh of relief. I hurried back upstairs to collect our bags.

From then on, Mum was compliant. She believed that Dad would be sailing with us. I knew it was improbable, as the instructions I'd received had made it clear that apart from the severely injured, no men would be permitted to join the ship.

We made our way through the chaos, towards the harbour. Walking along streets with bomb-damaged buildings, sandbags piled in doorways and broken glass everywhere, it was like a scene from newsreels of the London Blitz. We may have come late into this war, and extremely ill-prepared for it, but its presence was now incontrovertible. Just weeks before, the city of Singapore had been operating as 'business as usual' – no blackout, no drills, no fear. It was apparent that our days as lotus eaters in a tropical paradise were gone – possibly forever.

The docks had been laid waste. Where once godowns had lined the quay, there were piles of rubble, still smoking from the latest attack. The sky was black with the smoke from burning fuel and the fumes caught in my throat so that I struggled not to be sick.

At the dockside, a cargo ship, the *Empire Star,* was preparing to depart, already full to the gunwales with passengers, many of them nurses from the Alexandra. Around it, the quay was stacked with discharged cargo.

Mostly munitions and military supplies, there no longer being any warehouses to store them nor dock workers to move them. I couldn't help thinking that it was a pointless delivery and would probably have to be destroyed by the army before the Japanese could get their hands on it.

We were directed into a long line of people waiting to board another ship. As we stood waiting, a motorcar approached, pulling up at the far end of the harbour front, facing the water. Two men got out and together pushed the vehicle over the side of the quay into the water. It looked a new model. Smart. Expensive. American.

'Better than leaving it for the enemy,' Veronica said.

Just before dark, we were told we could board our waiting ship, moored beside the *Empire Star*. The *Royal Crown* was smaller, a passenger steamer that had been chartered by the admiralty for war use. It was being readied to transport women, children and wounded to Batavia in the Dutch East Indies, from where we would be travelling onward to safety in Australia, Ceylon or India.

Mum was bound to make another scene as soon as she found out Dad would not be coming. But Dad had anticipated this and took her aside to explain that he would be boarding separately, as the crew wanted to get the women and children settled first. Mum appeared to accept what she believed would be a brief separation.

I didn't know what to do. I felt duplicitous keeping the truth from Mum but the rules had been made clear. Women, children and wounded only. Dad would have to fend for himself.

Mindful that I might never see Dad again, I planned to stand on the deck and wave to him until he was out of sight, but he must have known this was possibly our last goodbye.

With a knowing look and a finger to his lips, he pushed a letter addressed to my mother into my hands, and once he saw we were safely up the gangplank, he turned and hurried away from the dockside. I didn't know it, but it would prove to be the last time I saw him.

3

INTO CAPTIVITY

Once on board the *Royal Crown*, I discovered that there were several deserting Australian soldiers who had managed to sneak aboard. I was angry. Dad was getting on in age and just a lowly bank official. He was not as strong as he used to be, and these soldiers were hale and hearty. There were also other men, managers from The Ministry of Works who had been evacuated with us. I failed to understand why they had been allowed to leave when men like Dad and Reggie Hyde-Underwood had been left behind.

The *Empire Star* left before us, slipping out of Keppel Harbour, with two-and-a-half-thousand passengers tightly crammed on board, as soon as daylight allowed them to negotiate the mines the British navy had laid through the southern approaches to the island. It was a choice between using daylight to navigate the minefield safely or using the cover of night to try to avoid the Japanese air attacks. Daylight sailing was judged the lesser risk.

Most of the women, including my mother, and all the children, were sent below to the hold where they would be safer from an aerial attack. Mum was dazed but happy to have found some friends from Penang among the throng and went compliantly into the hold as instructed. She was still nursing the belief that Dad was safely aboard, segregated from us.

As VADs, Veronica and I remained on deck with the wounded men and the nurses, so that we could assist where required and carry messages around the ship.

Just after nine that morning, the Japanese launched an attack on the *Empire Star*. Scores of planes, like a swarm of locusts, dived through the sky, relentlessly strafing and bombing the ship. On the decks of the *Royal Crown* we watched at a distance, helpless, at the other, larger ship under fire.

'They must know it's a ship of evacuees,' I said to Veronica who was standing beside me. 'It's sheer cruelty.' I ought to have lost the capacity to be surprised by such things.

'They don't care. All they want is to make us so demoralised we'll surrender as fast as possible.' Veronica's brow was furrowed, and I reflected how much she had changed since the war had caught up with us.

As we sailed away from the colony, I looked back at a sky red with the flames from burning buildings and oil tanks. The air was rent with the echo of shellfire and explosions. Singapore had become the yawning maw of hell.

This Armageddon was hard to reconcile with the familiar city of elegant colonial architecture. Abandoned were the tennis courts, the golf tournaments, the sun umbrellas dotted along the beach at the Singapore Swimming Club, the tea dances, parties and concerts, the fine dining and sipping of cocktails in the hotels and clubs. Singapore was in its death throes, laid waste by an army whose strategic battle planning contrasted sharply with our British incompetence and complacency.

As we passed into the open straits, our turn came. The whining screech of the diving Japanese planes competed with the screaming of children and their terrified mothers, huddled in the hold. Hearing, feeling, but not seeing an enemy attack, must have been even worse than watching it unfold.

I was busy helping the wounded men on the decks. The QAs had set up a makeshift nursing station and Veronica and I rushed about, fetching and carrying, cutting bandages and replacing simple dressings.

We appeared to be more fortunate than the other ship. The attack on us was brief and did no damage to the hull and the precious cargo in the hold. Just one short sally by half-a-dozen planes, depositing their remaining ammunition upon us after the full-scale attack on our sister ship – but plenty of damage was done. The servicemen sitting or stretchered on the deck, were open targets for the diving fighter planes, which sent burning white-hot shrapnel among them, unleashing even more injuries from breaking glass and flying splinters. Through it all, those men sat patiently, passing around the bottles of whisky someone had salvaged from the bar of the Singapore Club. A group of Australian and British airmen led a rousing chorus of *Waltzing Matilda*.

Two men and one nurse lost their lives in the short bombardment and their bodies were quietly slipped over the side while an army pastor said prayers. There was no possibility of keeping the bodies on board our overcrowded craft.

I had no time to think about anything, as I did the nurses' bidding, helping where possible, despite my lack of training or skills, until one of the sisters suggested that, as a teacher, I might be more use down in the hold where the children were in a state of abject terror.

ANY THOUGHTS I'd had of setting up an impromptu school-room for the children in the hold were soon dashed. People were squeezed tightly into the limited space, mothers clinging to small children and babies, all near hysterical with fright – even though the aerial attack had stopped.

Instead, I tried to get them to follow the example of the servicemen on deck, by singing. At first, there were only one or two participants, but after a few minutes, more joined in, along with several mothers, grateful for distraction. We worked our way through the complete canon of nursery rhymes and lullabies, before moving onto hymns and other songs. The tunes wandered off-key at times, but were soon steered back. Among the women were one or two I recog-nised from Penang – mainstays of the dramatic society and the choir.

We sailed on through the day, until early in the evening, without warning, the ship's engines went silent and we came to a sudden juddering halt.

For a moment there was deathly silence. My stomach did a somersault as fear gripped me. The children began to cry again.

I was sitting closest to the hatch leading to the compan-ionway. Jumping to my feet, I called, 'Keep on singing, chil-dren! I'll go and find out how long we're stopping here.'

I plastered a big grin across my face, but the blood in my veins was cold with fear. I went above to investigate.

Up on deck, even though it was after dark, the light was

white and intense. I blinked, temporarily blinded by the glare. The source was a pair of giant searchlights trained upon the *Royal Crown* by a Japanese warship. My heart stopped and I could feel my legs shaking.

Our captain had already run up a white flag to surrender the ship and signal the presence of women and children. I was frozen with terror at what lay ahead of us, as the air was split by strident barked orders conveyed over a loud hailer from the enemy vessel.

My legs shook so badly they could barely support my body. I wanted to stay on deck and witness what was about to happen, but I knew I had to find Mum first.

There was pandemonium in the hold. I stood in front of the hatchway and summoning up as much authority as I could muster, I told them all they needed to be extremely quiet. To my surprise they immediately shut up. The fear that was coursing through my body must have somehow been transmitted in my voice. Only one or two small babies continued to cry but everyone else looked at me expectantly.

I turned to an elderly woman who was sitting nearest to me. She had a fierce-looking countenance that I judged likely to inspire respect. 'I need to talk to my mum for a few minutes. Can you hold the fort?'

I guided Mum through the hatch into the companion-way, dreading breaking the news that we were prisoners of the Japanese – but telling her did not go in a way I would have predicted.

Mum took the news with equanimity. By now, the thud of feet and high-pitched voices coming from above us indicated that some of the Japanese had already come aboard.

'We'll just have to make the best of it,' she said, matter of factly. 'It won't be long before we're rescued and there are rules about how they have to treat us.' She folded her arms and looked defiant.

Relief surged through me. If she had behaved the way she had done in our last days in Singapore I couldn't have coped.

Mum's widowed friend, Marjorie Nolan, emerged into the corridor looking as brash and confident as Mum was. The two were evidently feeding off each other in the bravado stakes.

When Mum told her what was happening, Marjorie said, 'We'll show the Nips what British pluck is,' puffing up her large, shelf-like chest, like a bird in a mating ritual.

At that moment, three Japanese soldiers appeared at the end of the passageway. In front of them, his hands up, was the ship's captain. They screamed at Mum, Marjorie and me, and using their guns, on which the bayonets were primed and ready, they indicated we were to return to the hold. They pushed the captain in front of them, bundling him into the hold behind us. The hatch slammed shut.

Inside, the screams and cries began again.

The captain raised a hand and signaled everyone to be quiet. 'I have surrendered the ship into the hands of the enemy. We are now in the custody of the Japanese. Please stay calm and everything will be all right. I made the decision to surrender, as it is my first responsibility to ensure your safety, ladies. We are being taken to the nearest port where we will be disembarked and taken to a place to stay.'

The faces of the women telegraphed their shock.

The captain spoke again. 'They will likely arrest all the men onboard, but I am sure they will allow you and your children to go free as soon as we are on dry land. Please be patient until then and cooperate with any instructions you receive.'

When he had finished speaking, Mum turned to me. 'I have to find your father. I need to speak to him. If they are going to arrest the men. I must see him.'

Mum's new indomitability crumbled when I finally had to admit to her that Dad wasn't on the ship.

'You lied to me!' she shrieked. 'You said he was coming on board with the other men.'

'I had no choice, Mum. None of the men, apart from the wounded, were permitted to leave until all the women and children were evacuated. Dad understood that.' I reached into the pocket of my dress and pulled out the letter he had handed to me on the quayside. 'He asked me to give you this.'

I've no idea what my father had written to her and it was not my place to enquire, but Mum read that letter over and over again and, after weeping silently, folded it and put it into her handbag.

From that day on, Mum never complained about Dad's absence again, although she and I would speak of him often, wondering what he was doing.

I now know how lucky we were that day. Later, I would hear of other vessels – also with a cargo of evacuees – which were subjected to a sustained attack with massive loss of life. The Japanese appeared to have an aversion to taking prisoners, often preferring to put them to death. I suppose they wanted neither the cost nor the distraction of dealing with them.

After the war, I came to hear of numerous atrocities perpetrated against nurses, doctors and civilian women. Wounded men were bayoneted to death. Nurses raped and murdered as they went about their duties – and two Australian nurses I had known from the Singapore hospital wards were among those evacuated on the *Vyner Brooke*.

They were shipwrecked and survived the ordeal, only to be butchered by the Japanese when they came ashore at Radji Beach. I don't know whether my two colleagues were among those ordered to wade into the sea where they were machine-gunned to death, their blood turning the waves red, or whether they were among those still on the beach tending to the sick and dying, as the Japanese soldiers moved among them, driving bayonets through their helpless bodies.

I have often asked myself whether it might have been better to have been shipwrecked like several other evacuation ships. To be one of the women drowned, eaten by sharks, or dead from lack of water and exposure to the burning sun while clinging desperately to a life raft. That was the fate of the nurses and the women and the children they tried to save when another ship which left just hours before us was attacked, sunk, and abandoned off Pom Pong Island. The surviving women and children were rescued by a Dutch cruiser only for that to be shelled and sunk by the Japanese. The hold where they were housed took a direct hit. The nurses up on deck rescued as many as possible but after days at sea only one survived. Later I would meet her in the camp at Banka Island.

The *Empire Star*, in spite of enduring a sustained aerial attack, managed to limp its way to Batavia, from where, after repairs, the evacuees made it to Fremantle in Western Australia. For us on the *Royal Crown,* our war and our long suffering were only beginning.

4

BANKA ISLAND

The *Royal Crown,* under the control of our captors, followed behind the Japanese destroyer to Banka Island in Sumatra.

The Straits of Malacca are studded with a vast number of islands of varying sizes. Banka is one of the larger ones, hugging the coast at the end of Sumatra, about halfway between Singapore and Batavia in Java.

We came ashore a bedraggled mob, after our cramped passage in the hold of the ship and were marched along an extremely long pier to the shore.

Once on dry land, we got our first close-up sight of the enemy. They surveyed us with contempt, as though we were vermin.

This was a terrible shock to many of the British *mems* such as Marjorie Nolan, who were used to what they referred to as 'little Asiatics' running around doing their bidding. Here the roles were reversed and these men, battle-hardened from their years fighting in China, made that clear.

The Japanese soldiers paraded us in lines on the foreshore and ordered us to hand over our rings and watches. I managed to slip off my engagement ring and tuck it inside my brassière. I nudged Mum to do the same, but her wedding ring was trapped on her swollen finger. Fortunately, the Japanese took her wristwatch without noticing the ring.

'One bag only!' The guard snapped out his order in Japanese and a translator repeated it.

The one or two women foolish enough to try to debate this ruling were treated to a kick in the shins. Some, with two or more suitcases, were forced to make difficult choices. Most selected their biggest and heaviest case.

We looked about us, expecting to see buses to take us to our destination. After some time, I realised there was to be no transport. Wherever we were heading it would be on foot.

Once we got underway it became apparent our route was straight through the jungle.

'Thank heavens for hospital footwear,' I said to Mum, pointing to my sensible shoes. To my relief, she was wearing a pair of flats. But they were open sandals and her feet were soon muddy, scratched by undergrowth and bitten by insects, as we tramped through steaming rain-soaked jungle.

As Mum and I trudged along I had cause to be grateful for the advice Veronica had proffered in the hotel bedroom, to bring only a hold-all each. All around women were moaning and sighing as they struggled to carry heavy leather suitcases, filled to capacity. Marjorie was one of them.

'I simply can't go on. How can I be expected to carry a case as large as this one?' she asked.

'I did tell you to go for the smaller one,' Mum snapped at her friend.

'Who knows how long it will be before we get home. How could I possibly manage without sufficient changes of clothes? What do you take me for, Janet? Some of us believe in keeping up standards.' She sniffed pointedly. 'We have to fly the flag.' Ten minutes later, she let out a loud groan and dropped her suitcase on the ground.

Mum nudged me. 'Give her a hand, Mary.'

Biting my tongue and telling myself I was doing it for Mum, not for her ghastly friend, I stretched out my hand to take hold of the case. I had intended it as a swap for my much lighter hold-all, but Marjorie strode past me. 'Thank you, dear,' she called over her shoulder.

The suitcase weighed a ton.

Veronica appeared beside me and picked up my hold-all in her free hand. 'We'll take it in turns,' she said. 'We can switch every fifteen minutes or so.'

If my mouth was wide open in surprise Veronica didn't react. She gave me a tight little smile and raised her eyebrows. 'Rule Britannia,' she said, nodding her head in the direction of Marjorie's retreating bulk.

Yet carrying a heavy case was preferable, compared to those women clad in high heels. They looked like they were heading to a social function. By the time we reached our destination, several hours later, bleeding from our blisters, many had decided that bare feet was the lesser of two evils in spite of the proliferation of insects, sharp thorns and rough stony ground.

Our first abode was a place called Muntok Camp. To refer to it as accommodation is an enormous exaggeration. Muntok was a terrible place.

As soon as Marjorie saw the grim stone buildings where

we were expected to sleep on raised concrete platforms, she drew herself up to her full height and went into battle. 'This is completely unacceptable. Do they think we are animals?'

She approached the officer-in-charge and barked at him as if he were a servant caught in a misdemeanour. 'Are you the senior officer?'

The soldier stared back at her, his eyes cold and narrow behind the ubiquitous round-framed spectacles so many of the Japanese wore.

'This accommodation is utterly unsuitable. It just won't do.' Her tone was imperious, probably no different from the one she would have used to her cook or her *syce*. 'My husband is a high-ranking government official. You must find us an appropriate alternative immediately–'

The officer lashed his hand across her face with such force that we could hear the impact. His mouth formed a snarl and he screamed something to the men around him, striking terror in all of us.

One of Marjorie's teeth and all of her plucky fighting spirit deserted her and she began to cry. Her hand went up to her cheek which was livid red. Her lips were stained with blood from her gum.

That one blow demonstrated the new order. Servant was now master and we were to be under no illusions that we would receive any concession to status or gender. The age-old British colonial caste and class system with all its rules and conventions had been swept away in one angry slap of a hand.

To her credit and my surprise, my mother made no complaint about our conditions at Muntok, even to me in private – although she would have been perfectly justified in doing so. Marjorie's treatment had shocked us all and no one else raised any objections.

The camp had been built to house coolies working in the Dutch-owned tin mines. I hope those men had received better treatment there than we did, even though labouring in a tin mine must have been a thoroughly unpleasant experience. At least they'd have been properly fed.

The camp buildings were in a large horseshoe configuration. Our block housed women and children only, with another opposite where male prisoners of war were already in residence. The linking section of the U-shape was used by the Japanese guards. The place was spartan in the extreme – just an empty room with an *atap* roof, stone walls and those concrete sleeping slabs. We were given no bedding. The roof was in poor condition and the rain was pouring through as we walked into our new 'home'. The allotted space we each had for sleeping was about two-feet wide. Forty of us crammed into a dormitory intended for twenty coolies.

Sleeping was impossible that first night. As well as the noise of crying children, whispered conversations and snoring, the concrete sleeping slabs sloped downwards, so during the night gravity would send us sliding towards the floor.

That first day we had nothing to eat for twenty-four hours, presumably as a punishment for Marjorie's outburst. Inevitably, the smaller children, who were already confused and distressed, began wailing and crying with hunger. When eventually, we were fed the next day, it was only small bowls of rice.

The hungry children's distress was made worse when one of the guards chose to deal with it by hitting the small offenders on the shins with the butt of his rifle. None of the other soldiers or officers made any attempt to reprimand him for this and the rest of us were shocked into silence.

At the end of the room was a tap, fed by a metal water

tank, where we were expected to wash, although the same water was used to wash clothes and was dirty from the bodies of all who had washed before. Beyond was a small room with a line of squat latrines. Outside, in the area between ours and the men's block, was a roofed-over area with benches – the only seating in the camp.

I still nursed the hope that the captain of the *Royal Crown* was right, and the Japanese would eventually allow the women and children to go free. This hope was reinforced by the fact that the camp was already well over-capacity yet more and more people were admitted as the days passed. Surely it was impractical to keep us all. There were captured Dutch and British servicemen, including wounded soldiers from the *Kuala,* which had been sunk in an air attack, local Dutch families and evacuees from other captured or wrecked ships. One of the male prisoners told me that the local Muntok town prison was also filled beyond capacity. It was extraordinary to incarcerate the entire European and Eurasian civilian population of Malaya, Singapore, and the Dutch East Indies. Even had they thought the men, if left at liberty, represented a threat, it was cruel and unnecessary to imprison women and innocent children – some of them babies.

Water in the washing tank had to be replenished each day by hauling buckets from wells on the periphery of the encampment. Clothes washing was fraught with anxiety as it necessitated a close eye on drying laundry because the lack of garments among many of the inmates meant theft was not uncommon.

One day I came upon Mum having a huddled conversation with her Penang friends.

Marjorie was holding forth. 'I am absolutely certain it was her,' she said.

The others looked embarrassed and my mum said, 'What makes you so sure, Marjorie?'

'Sure about what?' I asked.

Mum looked at me apologetically. 'Marjorie thinks Mrs Leighton stole some of her underwear.'

'Thinks? Knows!' Marjorie pursed her lips.

I started to laugh. The idea of Veronica Leighton stealing underwear was bizarre – but that it should be that of the rotund Marjorie was beyond credibility. 'Mrs Leighton would never fit into your undergarments,' I said trying to suppress the giggles as I imagined the tiny sylph-like Veronica trying on the voluminous knickers that I had seen Marjorie hanging on the line that morning.

'I didn't mean she plans to wear them herself. But she might be planning to sell them or cut them up and make some for herself.'

I rolled my eyes. 'Might be? Did you see her take them?'

Marjorie jerked her head. 'She was in the vicinity just before I noticed they were gone.'

'Look,' I said, sweeping my arm around the crowded camp. 'Any of these people could have stolen your undergarments. Unless you have some solid evidence, I wouldn't recommend throwing blind accusations out.'

Giving me a look that would have soured milk, Marjorie huffed loudly but said no more.

The nurses were kept busy by the numerous ailments we had arrived with at the camp. Those who had been shipwrecked suffered from exposure and sunburn. Many had lacerated and blistered hands from hanging onto ship's ropes for hours while in the sea. There were torn feet, infected insect bites and blisters from the march to the camp. On top of these recent injuries, there was the challenge of treating long-term conditions without medicines, as well as the growing occurrence of malaria, dysentery and stomach upsets.

But the medical emergency that shocked us all was the plight of an RAF officer who had shattered both his feet. He was in excruciating pain, fading in and out of consciousness, and I hoped he couldn't hear the conference between the doctors and nurses present.

'We have to amputate that foot.' The speaker was a military doctor.

I closed my eyes at the thought of the poor chap and how the loss of a foot would affect his future. When I heard the doctor's next words I wanted to throw up.

'The Japs won't move him to the hospital and they won't let us have any instruments or anaesthesia.'

A collective gasp from the nurses went up.

'What will we do?' The speaker was an Australian nurse.

'Improvise.'

I will never forget the bravery of that poor wretched flight lieutenant. The doctors used a saw fashioned from the metal hoop of a barrel, with his pain numbed only by a small quantity of morphine. A few days later, it was decided he must lose the other foot too. But all his bravery was to no avail as he died soon after.

As I prayed for the soul of the dead flight lieutenant, I was grateful that Frank hadn't fallen into Japanese hands and would have had a quick death. If it had been he who had had to go through that ordeal, only to die anyway, I would not have been able to go on living.

I also remembered Doug Barrington, Evie's husband, who had died of septicaemia after refusing to have his leg amputated in a clean modern hospital. His obstinate refusal struck me as ungrateful and selfish in comparison with the ordeal of the dead airman.

From our earliest days in Muntok the cruelty of the guards was evident. With rare exceptions they were brutal and sadistic in a breathtakingly casual way. Whether it was a howling child or a woman who dared to answer back made no difference. Any minor infraction was a cue for a face slap at full force, a beating with a rifle butt or a kicking. They strutted around the camp with naked bayonets, and I had no doubt they would be all too ready to use them.

The Japanese were evidently unaccustomed to women answering back or speaking out – it seemed to go against all their expectations and sensibilities. We all learnt rapidly that it was unwise to provoke them – and we each had the scars and bruises to show for our defiance.

But it wasn't just the harsh conditions that rendered Muntok Camp a horrible place. There was something about the atmosphere there. Something that went beyond our imprisonment. I'm not being fanciful, as others said the same. Perhaps there was already something in the history of the place. Even though the surrounding jungle was rich and verdant, birds chorused in the treetops, and the sun shone down on a landscape similar to those I had come to love in Penang, there was something sinister, unsettling and malign about Muntok Camp. Although we knew the sky and jungle were out there, we could see little of them. There was just a narrow strip of sky visible between the huddled buildings, and this reinforced our sense of isolation from the rest of humanity. That strip of sky was not enough to offer us relief from the burning sun when we had to stand beneath it, but it offered us no perspective of the wider world.

One of the routines forced upon every prisoner in every internment and military POW camp throughout the growing Japanese empire was the daily roll call we came to know as *tenko*. While every POW camp everywhere has an understandable requirement to check that all inmates are present and no one has managed to escape, the Japanese version was custom-made to extract the highest level of humiliation. We were compelled to stand in line under the blazing sun at least once every day – or as often as our tormentors saw fit – and perform a kind of *kowtow* to them. Our bows of obeisance had to be as low and deep as possible – literally bending on a ninety-degree angle at the waist, with our arms at our sides. For older women and the sick this was a terrible ordeal. My mother, who suffered with her joints, was often breathless, and when she entered captivity was overweight, found the bowing onerous. There were others who initially resisted this ritual humiliation and near deification of our captors – until they were beaten so viciously that they were compelled to comply.

Our daily life at Muntok was harsh. The benches in the central covered area were insufficient to accommodate our growing numbers, and there was little or no natural shade, so we often had to sit on the floor or the concrete slabs of the huts. Plagues of flies and mosquitoes added to our ills, aiding the spread of disease and causing many to suffer badly infected bites.

Those of us who had arrived on the *Royal Crown* were more fortunate than the women who had been ship-wrecked. We had the possessions that we'd carried on our trek through the jungle. The others had only the clothes they stood up in, often stained with engine oil, stiff from sea water and in tatters. We became adept at creative solutions to clothing shortages. The most pressing problem of lack of protection from the fierce tropical sun was solved by making hats and footwear from straw matting or banana leaves.

One morning I awoke to Veronica shaking my shoulder. 'The latrines are overflowing,' she said, folding her arms and wrinkling her nose in disgust. 'The stench is foul. We're going to have to empty them.'

I gagged at the thought.

'There are too many people in here. It's inhumane,' Marjorie chipped in, her voice full of righteous indignation.

'I've spoken to one of the guards. We're going to have to do it ourselves,' added Veronica.

'We need to do it soon. It's already pouring over the sides. It's a serious health hazard.' The speaker was an Australian nurse. 'We'll have to draw up a rota.'

Marjorie was about to protest, when Mum put a hand on her arm. 'I'll volunteer,' she said.

Shocked at her friend, Marjorie shook her head in disbelief. 'Janet! You can't be serious? You're on your own then.' She curled up her lip and grimaced her disgust.

'We'll all do our bit,' Veronica said, pointedly. 'We all contribute to the problem so we can all deal with the solution.'

I overcame my squeamishness and added my name.

Every morning, we had to use whatever containers were available to scoop out the foul-smelling contents of the toilets, carry them across the camp and dump them outside the perimeter fence, while the Japs kept their guns trained on us in case anyone should attempt escape.

Marjorie had reluctantly agreed to be included in the rota – but I never actually saw her undertake any of the work.

KEEPING the children amused was another challenge. The Japanese strictly forbade any form of schooling or possession of pencils and paper, so, with a young nun, I had to exercise ingenuity to find ways to keep them occupied and learning something. Mostly this took the form of telling stories. The smallest children were too young to understand what was happening to them – why they were separated from their daddies, why they were in this terrible place with no food, no beds, no toys, no *amah* to care for them. As long as I live, I will never forgive the cruelty of making so many innocent children spend their most tender years under a reign of terror and deprivation.

Our stay at Muntok was not to be a long one. When we had been in the camp for about a month, it was decided to designate it as a POW camp for servicemen. Our future was to be elsewhere – in a camp on the main island of Dutch Sumatra.

5

A HOUSE BUT NOT A HOME

arch 1942
We had been at the camp for less than three weeks when we were woken at three o'clock in the morning and ordered to assemble. Everyone, except for the most gravely ill and some of the nurses, was given a handful of rice wrapped in a banana skin, and we set off in a crocodile to walk back through the jungle to the jetty. There, after walking its interminable length carrying our personal goods, we were packed onto an ancient rusting freight boat to depart for the main island of Sumatra.

I was sitting, on the deck, knees bent, Mum beside me, when someone tapped my shoulder.

'Look,' Veronica said, her voice uncharacteristically soft. 'Have you ever seen such a beautiful sunrise?'

I turned to look eastward. It was breathtaking, suffused with pink, turning to a brilliant orange close to the line where the sea met the sky. The reflected light of the sun shone onto the water, creating a spear of fire cutting through the surface to meet our craft. Beyond, and in contrast, the dark grey striations of the Straits of Malacca were broken by the black silhouettes of rocks and small islets. Vast sweeps of cloud raced towards us, lowering the ceiling of the sky. Edged with black, their centres took on the colour of the rising sun. It had rained torrentially before dawn and a rainbow arced above the water to greet the rising sun.

It struck me as deeply ironic that we were witnessing a vision that reflected the majesty of God and the artistry of nature, just as we were facing such suffering, cruelty and deprivation. Perhaps this was God's joke? Didn't the Japanese refer to their homeland as the land of the rising sun? It was the symbol of their national flag. Was God sending us a message with this celestial display? Was our subjugation a divine punishment? Retribution for past wrongs?

Seeing the tousled heads of the small children in our ragtag mob, I told myself that had to be wrong. Those children had done nothing to deserve their incarceration. The brave British and Australian nurses had done nothing but good and had selflessly helped others, working tirelessly to support those who were sick.

No. I decided to interpret the scene before me as a reminder of the need to maintain hope, to put my faith and trust in God and my own resilience. I would take all this heart-stopping beauty as a sign that, one day, life would begin again for us. One day, we might again enjoy freedom. In the meantime, I must hold onto hope, draw strength from it, and try to pass that strength on to help sustain my mother.

OUR ARRIVAL on the island of Sumatra marked a significant change in our surroundings. Instead of the spartan squalor of the coolie barracks, we were taken to occupy newly-built ordinary houses on an ordinary street.

If we were harbouring any hope that our situation was improving, we were soon disabused of it. Unlike the intended occupants – Dutch or Eurasian families – we were crammed into the small bungalows so that around twenty-five to thirty of us shared a space intended for a family of three or four. And the further bad news was that we were expected to remove any furniture and transport it on hand-carts, which we had to drag down the road ourselves, to furnish the houses where our captors would be living in significantly more comfort. This included cooking stoves, where any were present.

Mum and I ended up in a house with Veronica Leighton, Mum's friend Marjorie, half a dozen Dutch nuns who had been shipped in to join us from a convent in a nearby town, a gang of Australian nurses, a couple of Mum's and Marjorie's bridge cronies from Penang, a newly-married British couple, a Eurasian brother and sister who had lost their parents in a shipwreck, an elderly matron, Mrs Hopkins, and her unmarried daughter, Laura, who was about my age. Our complement was made up by a Dutch family, the Van den Boschs, consisting of husband, wife and three children, who were the rightful occupants of our new abode, and were less than thrilled about the transformation of their family home into a concentration camp.

One of the consequences of imprisonment was the throwing together of different nationalities and ethnic groupings. Our bungalow held a particularly diverse mix, as generally there had been a scurry for people to stay together, bagging space for friends. Back in our lives before the war, while Eurasians were tolerated by expatriate Euro-peans, an unvoiced hierarchy placed them a level below the

Europeans in the pecking order. Even among the Eurasians themselves, there were tensions between those of part Chinese origin and those of Malayan. But all the Eurasians saw themselves as superior to the indigenous peoples. Among the Europeans, the Dutch had been later arriving into captivity and hence had come prepared for it – better clothed and shod and with the funds with which to barter for food whenever opportunity arose. These Dutch people considered themselves a cut above the threadbare and penniless shipwrecked British and Australians.

Almost as soon as we moved into the house, the tensions began. Mr Van den Bosch insisted that he and his wife and children must retain what had been their bedroom and no one else was to be admitted. Needless to say, this immediately became a point of contention.

Marjorie was first into the fray. 'Look here, my good man. It is completely unreasonable for the four of you to expect to have exclusive use of the largest bedroom while two dozen of us have to sleep in two much smaller bedrooms and the living room.'

'This is my home,' he insisted, arms crossed over his chest in obstinate defiance.

'None of us has a home anymore, dear boy. We are all guests of these... these...terrible people. My home in Penang could well be a pile of rubble as far as I know.' She puffed out her chest, facing up to him. 'But I can assure you, Mr Van den Bosch, that it was a far grander residence than this place. In fact my servants' quarters were larger.' She gave an imperious sniff.

Outraged but outmanoeuvred, Mr Van den Bosch was offered two choices. One of the Australian nurses proposed that he and his family, if they wished to stay as a unit, might use what had served as their daughter's bedroom – little more than a box room. Faced with the alternative of sharing their original bedroom with the young British couple and three of the Dutch nuns, Mr Van den Bosch capitulated.

I was to sleep in what had been the sitting room. Our bedding consisted of straw mats on the tiled floor and some threadbare sheets. I shared this modest space with Mum, Marjorie and their two Penang friends – Daphne and Beryl, Veronica, Mrs Hopkins and Laura, and three of the nuns. The Australian nurses crammed into the former bedroom of the two Van den Bosch boys while the remaining nuns, the newly-weds and the Eurasian siblings took the main bedroom.

Triumphant over winning the battle of the bedrooms, Marjorie took it upon herself to assume the role of unelected Head of the house. I bet she'd been head girl at school. She gathered us all together in the area outside what had once been the kitchen, but now had only a sink and a single tap. This had been the garden, but was destined to be our cooking, eating and wood-chopping space. Using the kitchen for cooking was out of the question as we would need to build an open fire.

The first battle began almost immediately.

'We need a rota. If we identify what needs to be done each day, we can take it in turns to do each task.' Marjorie stood with her hands on her hips. 'I'll draw one up.'

'Not a good idea.' The naysayer was the newlywed husband, Terry Henderson who had been a clerk for the Ministry of Works. 'Better to allocate tasks according to capabilities. We have three men among us, and it makes sense that we take on the heavier jobs like chopping wood.' He glanced around him, looking for a reaction.

The Eurasian brother, who must have been about seventeen, nodded his agreement.

'Makes sense to me,' said Mr Van den Bosch, keen to support any proposal that was counter to Marjorie's.

Marjorie was seething. 'Not to me. Everyone should be trained to do all the necessary tasks. You never know when we may need to perform them. If someone is ill, someone else will need to pick up the slack.'

The nuns and nurses jumped in, supporting the men.

'I suspect we will have our hands full caring for the sick, but I for one am happy to pitch in with anything else if it's needed,' said one of the nurses.

'Why don't we start by identifying what the tasks are? Then we can decide how to allocate them.' The voice was my mother's.

I was surprised but encouraged. She had not shown much initiative since volunteering for the latrine clearing and had been in very low spirits while we were in Muntok. I think it was easier for her that we were in houses that, at least from the outside, had a semblance of normality, no longer in a penitential camp. Her intervention seemed to pacify Marjorie and distracted from her immediate loss of face.

As it happened, any illusion of normality was short-lived as, within days, lorries pulled up outside our row of houses and disgorged a cargo of barbed wire which local Indonesians were ordered to erect around the immediate area, thus separating us from the nearby town. While we had never been permitted to enter the town, the addition of this visible manifestation of our imprisonment had an immediate negative effect on morale.

We got into a regular pattern of activity. As in Muntok, we were up at six-thirty, and summoned to the daily roll call at eight. In between, we washed as best we could, using the single tap in what had been the kitchen – devoid of a cooker and most of its equipment, all appropriated by our oppressors.

The men chopped wood and we women took turns to prepare our breakfast of a tasteless gruel-like porridge made from ground up rice, washed down with 'coffee' – also made from the ubiquitous rice that was our staple diet. To make it, we burnt grains to provide the requisite brown colour, then boiled them in water. This rice-based diet was supplemented with vegetables when we could get them and – a rare treat – the very occasional inclusion of a scrap of meat. This would be scrupulously divided between us into tiny portions and had often been thrown to us by a guard, so we had to pick it up from the ground. Such behaviour by our captors was designed to make us feel like animals, degraded and humiliated. We all tried to rise above it, but it was hard not to let our spirits slip.

The inevitable bickering as we adjusted to living in such close proximity with people who had until recently been strangers, made adapting to the new regime even harder. In those first days, we had another territorial battle with the Van den Boschs. We had run out of fuel to heat the improvised stove we had created in the garden. To boil water, we used a large tin can suspended from a makeshift metal frame constructed by Terry, his wife and one of the nuns. Terry suggested removing the back door and using it for firewood.

'*Godverdomme!*' Mr Van den Bosch was red in the face. I spoke no Dutch, but it was apparent he was cursing. 'This is my home. *Houd je bek!* How dare you suggest burning my door you... you–'

Before he could finish his insult, Veronica stepped into the fray. 'Look, sir, no one is suggesting your door is sacrificed for their own benefit. It will ensure that we are *all* able to eat for the next few days – including your lovely wife and your delightful children. Unless, dear boy, you have some alternative source of fuel secreted away somewhere, I think it's time to do the decent thing.'

I don't think Mr Van den Bosch registered the heavy sarcasm in Veronica's reference to his wife and children, so dazzled was he by her smile. He looked over at his family, then nodded slowly in resignation.

This was how Veronica operated. She would remain quiet in the background and then make a small but significant intervention to resolve a problem. I found it hard to reconcile this practical and capable woman with the harpy I had known in Penang. I was coming to realise that captivity brought out the best and the worst in people. The war gave Veronica a sense of purpose she had lacked in peacetime, when she had filled her days with games of tennis, cocktail parties and gossip. Back then, she had been languid, often giving the impression of boredom. Despite its horrors, I am convinced she was more at home in internment than at liberty.

I saw my priority in the camp as being a support to Mum. I knew how frail she was and how hard she would be finding the separation from Dad. Until we left Penang ahead of him, I don't think Dad had ever been parted from her. I suspect he hadn't risen higher in the hierarchy in his career because of this. The few weeks he was out of touch while travelling to join us in Singapore had taken a heavy toll on Mum.

In our shared conversations we both set out to reassure each other and ourselves that Dad was thriving.

'What do you think your father's up to today?' Mum would say. 'I hope he's found himself a nice administrative role. All that trench-digging is no good at all for a man of his age.'

As the days became weeks and months, she persisted in this fantasy, in spite of the fact that not long after we were captured, while we were still at Banka Island, we'd heard the news that General Percival had surrendered Singapore in a humiliating manner and the European and most of the Eurasian population were now incarcerated as well.

Our scant rations were supplemented through the kindness of local Malays who, from time to time, would appear at the barbed wire and pass us their cast-off clothing and surplus vegetables. As we sat eating our meals around the improvised cooking pot, someone would inevitably say 'Not quite Raffles, but it will do,' or, as we sipped our ersatz burnt rice coffee, 'Standards are slipping at Robinson's, don't you think?'

Humour was an essential ingredient to our ability to sustain our *esprit de corps.* It also astonished and irritated the Japanese. We had been brought low, lost face and should have been consumed with so much shame that laughter would be impossible. Finding something, however trivial, to laugh at made life bearable, whether it was inventing silly names for our Japanese tormentors or playing up the irony in our situation.

In efforts to counter our see-the-funny-side-of-it demeanour, rumours, presumably initiated by the Japanese, began to circulate around the houses that made up our improvised detention camp. Until now I had no evidence, but I suspected Marjorie as being the culprit of spreading many of the rumours.

One morning I found Mum weeping. Marjorie was sitting on the floor beside her, arms folded.

'What's the matter?' I asked, looking at Marjorie with

suspicion. I had never been keen on the woman, finding her arrogant and selfish, and I guessed she was behind Mum's distress.

'Singapore has been razed to the ground and all the whites are dead,' said Mum between sniffs and sobs.

'What rubbish!' I countered, injecting as much confidence into the words as I could muster. 'That's propaganda. Why on earth would the Japs destroy the city they've wanted to get their hands on for so long?'

'But if they've killed all the white people that means ... your father will be...'

'Of course, they haven't killed all the white people. If they had, why would they be keeping us alive? And do you have any idea what it would take to systematically kill everyone left in Singapore?' I fixed my eyes on Marjorie, summoning up a stern expression. 'It's poppycock.'

'I had it on very good authority,' Marjorie put her hands on her hips and gave me a defiant look.

'Hirohito himself, I imagine. A chum of yours, is he?' I knew I was being unnecessarily catty, but I was furious with Marjorie. This kind of negative rumour-mongering would sap morale and play right into the hands of our captors. And I knew Marjorie was doing it to self-aggrandise. She liked nothing more than to be treated as the queen bee.

With a huff and a shrug of one shoulder, the woman walked away.

Another aspect of life in the Dutch houses, was the way the Japanese guards would enter the buildings without warning or invitation. They did this with no purpose other than to pry, often following us from room to room and standing in doorways to watch us dress or wash – by now all the internal doors had made it to the fuel pile. There was no point objecting as it made them worse, so we developed an ability to pretend they were not there. Many of these guards were little more than adolescents – peasant boys whose motivation to torment us in this way was curiosity rather than malevolence.

It was around this time that several of the women began disappearing, returning with food and money. In my naivety, I didn't realise what they were doing at first, until Veronica – who was one of them – enlightened me.

'If it's going to keep me better fed in this godforsaken place, I'll do it. Worse things can happen. And better to do it on my terms than on theirs,' she said. 'If none of us do, all of us will suffer. If the Japs want to ease their frustrations, it's better that some of us profit from it. If we don't, they'll take it by force from us all.'

I was horrified. That she, a married woman, albeit an unfaithful one, could so calmly prostitute herself to the enemy for a can of condensed milk or a few guilders. In those days, I was quick to judge.

Our good humour was further and more severely tested when out of the blue one morning, all the men in the camp, a small but significant minority, were ordered to line up in the street outside the houses. It became clear that they were about to be moved. While the men had been outnumbered by us women, their presence had been a psychological reassurance – even though we all knew they were as powerless as we were and could have done nothing to defend us. Among them were Mr Van den Bosch, Terry Henderson, Cyril Pickering – the Eurasian youth, and Mr Van den Bosch's older son, Geert, who was only twelve.

To my surprise, Mrs Van den Bosch took this separation in her stride. She stood stoically, one hand on the shoulders of each of her two remaining children, as her husband and son were led away. This wasn't the case with either Sharon

Henderson, Terry's wife, or the Eurasian girl, whose name was Cynthia Pickering. Sharon cried big gulping tears, unable to comprehend that her husband of just weeks was being taken from her. Laura and Mrs Hopkins rushed over to support her as she swayed, about to faint.

No one did this for Cynthia, who fell to her knees, in abject desolation at being parted from her brother. It was Veronica who eventually went to her, helping her onto her feet, saying something I couldn't hear and taking Cynthia's hand and squeezing it.

I admit I stared open-mouthed at this development. For a woman I had always seen to be an arch snob, it was an egalitarian act – as well as one of kindness.

After the men had left, we gradually readjusted. Some, my mother among them, supplemented the house's meagre diet by earning money with which to barter for food. The source of the income was the Japanese themselves – but not in this case through prostitution. The guards' preferred attire, when not going about their official duties, was a kind of white loin cloth and they were prepared to pay us a pittance for these garments to be made. This was obviously neither a reliable nor a long-term source of income, but in those early days it offered a small means of contributing something, for those who had absolutely nothing.

Bartering with the locals was a dangerous risk. This was brought home to us in a terrible and frightening way one morning when a Malayan man was caught trying to attract our attention with a dead chicken he was holding against the wire fence. Fortunately, noticing that there were several Japanese in the vicinity, none of us approached him. Had anyone done so they may well have suffered the same fate he did. The guards took away the chicken, then, twisting his arms painfully behind him, they tied the man to a post just outside the perimeter fence and left him there for two days in the full blaze of the sun and the cold of the night. I cannot imagine the agonies that man must have suffered. We never discovered his ultimate fate because they took him away at the end of the second day. I suspect he was put to death.

OUR GUARDS no doubt felt humiliated that they were reduced to playing jailers to a collection of women and children, so they treated us with utter contempt. They screamed abuse at the *tenko* if we failed to make our bows low enough. As we became thinner and dirtier, they appeared to stop seeing us as women. Their eyes showed they despised our tall, white, emaciated bodies, our swollen "rice bellies" and our protuberant bones. To them we were a pointless species, unsuitable as pets, but needing to be held as captives. We were a drain on their resources, a distraction from the true purpose of war and their unfulfilled need to be fighting-men, advancing the glory of the empire and the humiliation of the white man.

They beat us, tortured us, treated us savagely and did everything they could to bring us low. They starved us of food and withheld the medicine we needed. Day by day they sapped our spirits and many women, accustomed to a life of expatriate ease, found our treatment unbearable. Later, as disease became more rampant and the effects of sustained malnutrition began to take their toll, these women were among the first to die.

Veronica was not one of these. She was different. In the beginning, the Japs seemed to see this too. It appeared they liked her, even respected her. She was small, slight, graceful, elfin. Not unlike a delicate Japanese geisha. When she flirted, they responded, not with the rifle butts they had used to beat other women, but with shy smiles and knowing grins. Veronica was smart. No one knew how she managed it, but she soon set herself apart from the rest of us. If she was going to have sex with the enemy, it was to be with Sergeant Shoei, the deputy to the camp commandant not with the rank and file guards, and it was done on her terms.

6

ADAPTING

In peacetime Mum had shown no inclination for singing or for music in general. Yet she became an enthusiastic member of the camp choir. Her pre-war interests had centred around regular bridge games, the voracious consumption of English detective novels, a daily crossword puzzle after breakfast, and baking. Easing aside our cook, Mum would take over the kitchen in a flurry of flour to make delicious scones, Victoria sponges and Dad's favourite flapjacks. The crossword puzzles, the supply of reading material and of course the baking, were no longer possible. Singing, on the other hand, was something that puzzled the Japanese, but which they felt powerless to prevent – and eventually came to grudgingly accept and even enjoy.

Mum and her friends also played bridge, two of them having happened to have packs of cards in their handbags, which escaped confiscation by the guards. They were soon in demand to pass on their card skills to eager learners, keen to find an occupation to distract from ailments and constant hunger.

'What were you and Marjorie up to this afternoon,' I asked Mum one day. 'You were huddled together hatching some kind of plot.'

'We've decided to create a cookbook,' she said, as if it were the most natural thing in the world. As though sharing recipes and tasting the results was the normal course of events in this terrible place of hunger and deprivation and we had writing materials, let alone ingredients for dishes.

I must have looked puzzled, worried even, because Mum rushed on, full of enthusiasm. 'It's just a bit of fun, love. Although it's a bit of a chore having to scratch all the recipes onto bits of roof tile, but Beryl has very tiny handwriting and she's in charge of recording it all. So far, we've done recipes for soup. We're about to go on to cakes and biscuits and I'm the editor-in-chief for that section.' She beamed with pride.

'What's the point? Surely it makes it worse thinking about food when we can't get hold of any?' I was incredulous. 'How can you possibly want to make a recipe book full of food you can't eat?'

'It's a vicarious pleasure, Mary. It reminds us of how things used to be and how they will be again. Yes, it's only a fantasy but believe me, it feels real. We start off by listing all the ingredients and then the method and everyone pictures the steps in their heads. The person who has offered the recipe has to describe the taste and feel and texture of the dish concerned, and we all sit around and pretend we're eating it.' She patted me on the arm. 'Remember my scones? They've proved quite a hit.'

'But, Mum...'

'Once all this is over, we're going to have regular get-togethers to eat our way through the whole cookbook. Can you imagine?'

She grinned but underneath the broad smile, I noticed how thin and drawn her once round face had become. I placed my palm gently against the soft skin of her cheek. Then I told her that one day soon we would both be eating her fruit scones, warm from the oven, butter melting and dripping down our chins. We laughed, then, looking sad, Mum turned away, hoping I hadn't noticed the tears at the corners of her eyes. I knew she was thinking about Dad and wondering whether she would ever see him again and whether we three would ever sit around the dining table together or share a sundowner in the garden before supper.

RUMOURS ABOUNDED IN THE CAMP. Whenever the Japanese were particularly vicious or angry with us, the word would race around between the houses that it was due to a significant military setback and that they were losing the war they had so confidently started. We had no concrete evidence for it. Imagination and rumour filled the void and helped to keep our spirits up.

This optimism about eventual victory was reinforced by the growing number of nationalities present in the camp. Besides British, Dutch, Eurasians and Australians, there were a couple of American missionaries, a Canadian nurse, French, Chinese, Malay, one Indian, an orphaned Russian child, two Italians and eventually a trio of Germans – for the Axis powers had never been as closely knit an alliance as the Allies were. Surely, with almost the entire world ranged against them, the small island nation of Japan could not prevail, and it was only a matter of time before we would be liberated.

Yet time is an odd commodity. On the one hand, it hung

heavily upon us, with hunger, hard labour and lack of enter-
tainment making our days drag. But it was also the enemy as
far as our health and wellbeing was concerned – as time
passed, we all became weaker – only the very strongest were
capable of marshalling the strength to stay alive.

Mum first became ill while we were living in the Dutch
houses. The flesh had fallen away from her and she suffered
badly from a series of ailments that we lacked the medicine
to treat. A bad bout of malaria saw her laid up for weeks and
it was thanks to Veronica, who managed to obtain some
quinine from an undeclared source, that she survived. But
the malaria left Mum weakened and even more vulnerable.

In the camp we were not generally sexually abused – the
Japs preferred the Malay and Chinese comfort women for
that, and those women who slipped away to service their
captors' needs before returning to camp.

Veronica had the unusual privilege of being the exclusive possession of the deputy camp commandant; their
encounters took place behind the closed door of his accommodation, in a bungalow outside the wire. She used this as a
means to smuggle in food and medicine whenever she
could. It was the kind of risk she appeared to relish.

For most of us the idea of prostituting ourselves for our
'masters' was unthinkable. I do not blame those who did
choose this course though. But Veronica's arrangement was
different.

Sergeant Shoei was the kind of man who would not be
happy to use the same women that his subordinates
accessed. He was also lazy and rarely left his house, other
than in fulfilment of his duties – which mainly consisted of
marching around shouting at his men and screaming at us.
Not for him the trip into the town to the house of prostitution where the 'comfort women' were kept.

For a long time, I believed that Veronica had recognised this as an opportunity to be the chosen candidate. Because I had always thought so badly of her, I assumed she had betrayed us by consorting with the enemy. I thought of her as little more than a prostitute anyway, after what had happened with Ralph and her callous abandonment of him. I was grateful for the medicines she brought back for my mother and others. But I still believed her real motives were entirely selfish.

Since the day her brother was separated from her, Cynthia Pickering spent every possible moment with Veronica, following her around like a devoted handmaiden and talking intently with her at any opportunity. It was an unlikely alliance – but Veronica had always operated with a posse of women friends in Penang. Not actually friends, but followers – women who preferred to stay on the right side of her. Cynthia, a quiet Eurasian girl, did not conform to the 'type' of Veronica's Penang posse – shallow, brittle women, obsessed with appearances, thriving on gossip and living to party.

It seemed to me a shame that a young innocent woman like Cynthia should fall under the corrupting spell of Veronica. I shuddered at the thought of her being encouraged to go down the same route and sell her body for a scrap of meat or a lipstick. But it wasn't my place to interfere. Cynthia was sixteen and old enough to choose her own friends, but I was sad that she was no longer under the protection of her adored older brother.

7

THE MEN'S CAMP

September 1943

We had been living in the Dutch houses for more than a year and had begun to settle into the harsh but manageable routine of life there. Out of the blue, we were told we would be moving the following day and must be ready to depart at three o'clock in the morning, with anything we wished to take with us. In fact, we had fewer possessions than when we arrived, our clothes having been worn to shreds. Anything of value, apart from one or two personal treasures, had already been consumed or bartered.

As always with these moves, we were given no information as to our destination or mode of travel. The idea of relocating filled us with anxiety. Human beings are capable of adapting to almost anything and we had become used to our peculiar suburban prison and recalled with horror those sloping concrete sleeping slabs we had known in Muntok.

'Where do you think they're taking us?' Mum's eyes were full of fear.

'Hopefully, they've built a proper place to house us,' said Marjorie. 'It had better be somewhere with decent dormitories and toilet facilities.'

While I thought that unlikely, I said nothing.

Mum looked bone-tired. 'I do hope we won't have to walk there. My feet couldn't take another trek through the jungle.'

As it happened, our next destination was less than a mile away – the camp the men had been occupying. It was absolutely awful. It had been built by the men themselves and, little knowing that the next occupants would be us women, they had sabotaged the place before they left, throwing rubbish into the wells, and causing destruction that made our lives even more uncomfortable than theirs had been.

The buildings were constructed from wood with roofs thatched with *atap*. Our arrival coincided with a spell of almost constant rainfall – heavy deluges of an apocalyptic nature that soaked through the thatch and made sleeping akin to taking a cold shower. One of the nuns had evidently missed her true vocation as a steeplejack, as she was constantly employed scrambling across the rooftops, her habit tucked into her waist, dragging the thatching back into position after the wind and rain had disturbed it.

Our guards had accompanied us to the new camp and their accommodation was in huts inside the perimeter. At this time, Veronica was continuing to service Sergeant Shoei.

'I don't understand how you can bear it,' I told her once. In the light of her continuing to supply the nursing staff with much-needed medicines, I didn't want to be disparaging or moralistic about her choice, but it was an unusual one among the married British women.

Veronica scuffed at the dusty ground with the edge of her foot. 'I don't like men. I don't enjoy doing it with any of them. Never have. So why not with him? It's all the same to me. And at least it makes life here a little easier for us.' She gave a dry laugh. 'Shoei is a monster but he'd be worse if I wasn't giving him what he wants, when he wants it.'

I stared at her, uncomprehending. 'But if you don't like doing it, why...?' I wanted to ask why she had slept with Ralph and made him fall in love with her, knowing full well that he had been engaged to marry me.

She gave a little shrug. 'It makes me feel there's a point to me – giving men pleasure. I used to think it was all I was good at. It was certainly the only time that I ever felt valued.' She paused, tilting her head back and staring up at the grey sky. 'You want to know why I seduced your fiancé, don't you?'

I nodded.

'You won't like it.' She stared right at me. 'I did it because you looked so damned happy. I saw you with him at some match. Cricket or rugby. I can't remember. I was feeling very low. I used to suffer from very black moods. Close to despair. Seeing other people happy made it worse.' She closed her eyes for a moment. 'And the only way I could make the pain feel better was to see other people suffering too. Funnily enough, since being locked up like this, I don't get those black spells anymore.'

I didn't know what to say. I was dumbfounded.

'It was nothing personal, Mary. I didn't even know you then. You kept yourself apart. Not one of the gang. I suppose that made you an easy target. I'm sorry. I never meant to be the cause of what happened. The boy killing himself.'

'He wasn't a boy,' I snapped.

'He was to me. I was fifteen years older than the poor chap.' She looked at me, her gaze intent. 'I thought he'd see it for what it was. A passing fancy. A brief affair. I wanted to hurt you, shake you up. I thought you'd make up eventually and carry on with your lives. I had no idea he'd commit suicide. It was just an unthinking desire to wipe the self-satisfied smile off your face.'

Before I knew what I was doing, I'd whipped my hand back and struck her across the face.

She put her own hand up to cup her reddened cheek. 'I asked for that, didn't I?'

I nodded but felt no triumph.

'Look, Mary, we've cleared the air. Let's forget about it. The RAF chap you were going to marry was twice the man Ralph was. I'm truly sorry he didn't make it.'

I snarled at her. 'Come off it, Veronica. You tried to make a pass at him too. At the Camerons' party at the Penang Club.'

'That was the drink talking. I used to have a problem in that department. Rather too fond of getting intoxicated.' She lit one of the cigarettes that were part of her booty from sleeping with the enemy. Veronica always used a lacquer cigarette holder and it was something she protected assiduously. Even here in the squalor of the camp it lent her an air of fashionable sophistication that her ragged clothes belied. 'Anyway, I'd have got absolutely nowhere. It was obvious even to someone as insensitive as I am, that Frank Hyde-Underwood worshipped the ground you walked on.'

That was it. For the first time since we had been imprisoned, I burst into tears.

Veronica wrapped an arm around me and held me as I sobbed into her shoulder.

Eventually she spoke again. 'It must be a miraculous thing to love and be loved by someone as much as that. You have a great capacity for love, Mary. It will come to you again.'

Sniffling, I wiped my hand across my nose. Handkerchiefs were long-forgotten luxuries. 'It won't. And I don't want it anyway. Love is all about pain and sorrow. And I'm cursed. Engaged twice and both men dead.'

She took my hand in hers. 'Not when you are loved in return. There was no pain and sorrow in your feelings for Frank. The pain and sorrow came from war not from love.' She looked into the middle distance, thoughtful. 'It's only now that I will probably never see him again that I realise how much I love my husband.'

'This war won't go on forever,' I said. 'You'll see him again.'

'I won't. I am certain of that. Our marriage is over anyway. Arthur never loved me. At least not in that way. Not as a husband should love his wife. He cared for me. I think he felt sorry for me. He was good to me. But having someone pity you is no recipe for a successful marriage. And certainly not now he's fallen in love with someone else.'

This was news to me. Arthur Leighton had always struck me as the devoted long-suffering husband, taking Veronica back after all her extra-marital adventures. 'Someone else? Who?'

But Veronica already clearly regretted that last confession. She got up and brushed her hands down the skirt of her faded threadbare frock and pulled back her shoulders. Even unwashed, with cropped hair and one filthy dress, Veronica had an air of elegance about her. 'No one you'd know,' she said briskly. 'It's time I got stuck into the rice-picking.'

She was not referring to a trip into the paddy fields but to the painstaking and fiddly process of picking through the rice rations. These were literally the sweepings off the factory floor, and in order to cook with them, they had to be sorted grain by grain, to remove the weevils, grit, glass, and dead insects. 'Cynthia will be wondering why I've abandoned her to the job.' She gave me a brittle smile and then she was gone.

NOT LONG AFTER we were installed in the new camp, I became aware that one of the guards was taking a lot of interest in me. He was new, presumably a leftover from the time of the men's occupation. I tried to ignore him and pretend it wasn't happening. But when he started following me every time I went to fetch water, I realised he wasn't just checking that I wouldn't try to make an escape.

The guard was young, probably only about eighteen or nineteen, and like most of the Japanese, myopic and wearing the ubiquitous round spectacles that I came to the conclusion must be army issue. His name was Tanaka and he had a broad, rather plump peasant-like face and didn't look as though he needed to shave often, if at all. We used to refer to him as Turnip Head.

Everywhere I went in the camp, the young man was either already there or not far behind me. Some of the other women noticed his puppy-like devotion to me and started making jokes about it. One day, one of the other guards, witnessing the way the women were joshing me, realised the source of the hilarity. He shouted something to my young shadow and the boy retreated. I was relieved. It had begun to annoy me.

About two days after the incident with the second guard, I was near the perimeter fence, searching for fallen twigs and branches to use as firewood. It was a secluded spot, away from the middle of the camp and I liked to be there as it was the only time I managed to be alone with my thoughts. Chopping wood with a kitchen knife was hard work. I was lethargic, due to the near starvation rations and the lack of variety in our diet.

That morning it had been raining heavily and the trees near the fence were dripping with rainwater. Standing beneath them to do the work meant that was I out of the full strength of the sun, and able to enjoy the odd cooling shower, as birds or a breeze disturbed the foliage and sent drops down upon me, cooling my neck as I bent to the task.

I sensed his presence before I saw him. Looking up, I saw Turnip Head was standing a short distance away, watching me intently. I gave him a polite smile – it was always best to try to stay on the right side of the guards and while this one had shown no aggression towards me, it was wise not to take any chances. I carried on splitting the wood.

It happened very quickly. Too fast for me to anticipate his attack. The knife was jerked from my hands and he threw it aside, then pushed me over so that I landed hard on my back on the bare ground. Before I could scramble up on my feet, he was upon me, grasping at my thin dress, pushing it up and using his knee to force open my legs. I cried out, but he pressed his small, pudgy hand over my mouth and straddled me. I could smell the sweat on him, pungent, stale, and his breath against my face was foul and sulphurous as though he had been eating eggs. I gagged. His well-fed, small-framed body weighed me down as I struggled to break free from under him.

No! My first sexual experience was not going to be a forced one and certainly not with an undersized, plump-faced Japanese boy, an uneducated peasant who wanted to slake his teenage lust on my unwilling body.

I sank my teeth into the smooth shiny skin of his cheek and he yelped in pain. I was about to take advantage of his surprise to push him off and make my escape, when I felt the cold point of a bayonet press against my neck. That was it. Rape was inevitable. Looking past my assailant I saw two other guards, standing, legs apart, their bayonets pointing at me. Laughing. One of them spoke rapidly to my attacker and with mounting horror and dread I knew they were goading their colleague on, taunting him to get the job done. One of them was thrusting his hips back and forth in a grotesque parody of the sex act.

I will not describe the details of what happened. Suffice to say that this pubescent soldier stole my virginity there on the hard, bare ground under the trees. The pain was terrible, and I prayed for it to be over. The two others were waiting to take their turn. They would finish me off with their bayonets when they were done. I would have welcomed the swift release of a bayonet in preference to the horror of what that boy-man was doing to me.

It was Veronica who saved me from the other guards and probable death. Later, she told me she had seen Turnip Head follow me and as soon as she noticed the two other men had gone after him, she guessed what was about to happen. From a distance, she saw him push me down onto the ground, so she went to fetch Sergeant Shoei.

As Tanaka finished his brutal invasion of my body, with a final violent thrust and a cry of triumph, he was yanked away by the collar. I opened my eyes. Sergeant Shoei was screaming at the three men and another guard was holding Turnip Head by the scruff of the neck. Tears spilled down my face and I struggled to get on my feet. As I stood up, blood trickled down my thigh, mingling with the sticky residue of the guard. I turned my head and vomited onto the hard-baked earth.

Shoei focused his attention on me, striking me hard across the face and screaming in Japanese. Then he swivelled on his heels and headed back across the camp, the other guards hurrying behind him.

AFTER THE RAPE, I sat slumped on the ground, bitter and angry. The casual way in which my body had been used for the instant gratification of a man filled me with disgust. I had been a vessel for him to satisfy his need for sexual release and if its attainment came at the cost of my virginity, my self-respect, physical distress and pain, it mattered not to him. I tried to be grateful that my ordeal had been curtailed by the arrival of Veronica with the deputy commandant but all I felt was sorrow and a deep feeling of shame.

This is why rape is such a potent and terrible weapon of war. For it is indeed a weapon, used indiscriminately by armies throughout history. Not only is there the physical pain and violence of the rape itself, the hatred and desire to debase, which the act represents – but there is also the shame it produces in the victim. I wanted no one to know. I wanted to crawl away and hide, to die, to disappear. The thought of my mother finding out was unbearable. I felt dirty, despoiled, ruined.

Veronica sensed this. We sat on the ground while she cradled my head in her lap and stroked my hair. It was generous, and uncharacteristic of the Veronica I thought I had known. Her usual response to adversity was to take control, boss people about, organise, fix things. Act first, explain later. Now, she was taking time to let me be. She gave me her presence; she bore witness to my pain but never once told me to pull myself together or offered empty platitudes.

I've no idea how long we sat there, silent, waiting. If she had led me back into the heart of the camp, placed me into the care of the nurses, made a fuss, told the others about what had happened, I would have probably lacked the strength to carry on.

'Thank you,' I said at last.

'There's no need to thank me.'

'If you hadn't appeared with Shoei they would all have taken a turn with me and killed me afterwards. There was no one to witness it. They'd have said I was trying to escape.'

'Probably,' she said, simply.

I looked towards the huts. I could hear the camp choir singing. 'You won't tell anyone, will you?'

'Not if you don't want me to.'

'I don't. And after today I'd rather you and I never mentioned it again.' I bit my lip. 'I don't want Mum to know what he did to me. She wouldn't take it well. She's depressed enough as it is.'

Veronica nodded.

'Do you think I will ever be able to forget this?'

She looked at me sharply, knowingly. 'No. You won't. Ever. But with time you'll be able to see it for what it was – an act of war, and something in which you yourself played no part and must carry no guilt. The only people who should feel shame at what happened to you are the man who did it and the men who watched. It doesn't make *you* a bad person.'

She let out a long sigh and fixed her eyes on mine. 'The only other person I have ever told what I am about to tell you, is my husband.' Looking away, she said, 'I was raped as a child. Twelve years old.'

I gasped, shocked. It was impossible to imagine the cool, aloof, elegant Veronica ever going through the trauma of what I had just experienced – and doing so while a child.

'Who did it to you?'

'That doesn't matter. It was so long ago. Let's just say he was one of my mother's gentlemen friends. A sailor. He was very rough with me. When he was done, I was so filled with shame I ran away. I vowed it would never happen again.' She narrowed her eyes and took a breath, drawing the air deep into her lungs. 'And it never has. I make sure I'm the one in control where men are concerned. Why do you think I made a play for Shoei? I want his protection. None of the others will dare to lay a finger on me.'

She gave a little snort. 'I loathe him with every fibre of my being. His horrible hairless bandy legs, his fat belly, his tiny hands. Most of the time I can get away with using only my hands to deal with him – and it's usually over quickly.' She gave a little chuckle. 'I suppose I should be thankful for small mercies.'

I didn't know what to say. I wasn't surprised by what she was revealing about the deputy commandant, but I was stunned by her girlhood trauma. It was hard to square the picture of that little girl with Veronica's sturdy resilience, her brazen self-confidence and her innate sense of social superiority. It was all an act – armour she girded herself with to face whatever obstacles were put in her path.

'How are you feeling?' she asked. 'Ready to face the world?'

I nodded and we went back to the camp.

To my relief, I never saw Turnip Head Tanaka again. Veronica told me later that Shoei had transferred him to one of the men's camps. After that, she and I never spoke again of what happened to me. Or of what had happened to her.

8

PENNY ARRIVES

November 1944

In the camp, children were not afforded any special treatment by our captors, but they were tolerated and some of the guards appeared to find them amusing, like small pets. It was rare these days that they would punish or strike a child. Children were not deemed to merit the same contempt their parents received, as members of the losing side. Since we had chosen not to do the honourable thing and ritually kill ourselves for the shame and disgrace of surrender, we were worthless, lower than mongrels and if we starved to death or succumbed to disease, so much the better.

Disease was rife. Every manner of sickness from the inevitable malaria and dysentery to malnutrition. All would have been easily treatable with medication. The only medicine we had in camp was what the nuns and nurses had managed to bring in with them – and later what Veronica managed to procure. This was another example of her selflessness. Instead of using the small sums of cash and supplies of cigarettes she got from Sergeant Shoei to buy and barter indulgences for herself, she kept only a modest amount of smokes and used everything else to exchange for food, which she shared, and where possible medicines. It was this that kept my mother going through almost constant bouts of malaria and dysentery. Later we were to discover that the Japanese had plentiful medical supplies in storage – including the contents of the Red Cross parcels which they neither distributed nor even told us existed.

One of the strange aspects of our long internment was the way the numbers in the camps continued to increase. In the earlier days it contributed to the unpleasant over-crowding and the severe limitations of our allotted sleeping space. In the later days, the new arrivals barely kept pace with the rate of dying.

The newcomers were sometimes recent 'acquisitions' by the Japanese – many of them Dutch, or Hollanders as they preferred to be known, who had been under house arrest in their own homes at first. Some were stragglers from various shipwrecks; one or two had been living in hiding under the protection of villagers. Some were brought in from other camps on the whim of our captors, who appeared to enjoy moving their detainees from camp to camp like pieces on a chess board. As there was no rhyme nor reason, I came to the conclusion it was a bureaucratic game – or possibly a power struggle between rival camp commandants. The Japanese appeared to have no love for each other; none of the sense of *esprit de corps* I had witnessed in our own servicemen and which, here in camp, was most apparent among the large group of Australian nurses and the Dutch nuns.

One day, almost six months after we had arrived in the former men's camp, a dozen new internees arrived and among them I saw a face I recognised. A scrawny-legged girl of about twelve or thirteen with large sad eyes. Alone.

Moving as fast as my weakened legs would carry me, I ran over to greet her. Penny Cameron had once been my pupil, my next door neighbours' child, and the best friend of Jasmine Barrington, Evie's daughter.

Feisty, mischievous, often outspoken, Penny had been a spirited little girl, yet as I looked into those huge saucer-like eyes, I could see only emptiness and despair.

'Penny!' I clutched her tight against me. 'I am so happy to see you.' That sounded wrong, so I added, 'Well, not in this place of course. I wish we were meeting somewhere else.'

'Miss Helston.' It was all she said. She was listless, as though she had no will to keep on living, but had already had enough of her all too brief life.

'How did you come to be here? Where are your parents?'

Her face was expressionless, revealing no emotion. 'We were on a ship that got bombed. Mummy was drowned. I don't know what happened to Daddy. He's probably dead too. There was a big explosion.'

I felt a surge of sorrow and anger on behalf of this little girl whose childhood had been wrested from her, who had seen so much suffering and grief at such a tender age. I held her against me, feeling her warm breath against the thin cotton of my dress. 'I'll take care of you, Penny. We'll get through this together, I promise you.'

As I comforted her, I wondered if the promise was within my power to keep. How could I be certain we'd survive? Every day, conditions in the camp got worse. The food situation was desperate, with our Japanese jailers making no attempt to provide us with the minimum necessary for survival. The funds afforded to the local suppliers of our paltry rations were constantly cut; the food needed to be stretched further and the portions became smaller. Every day, we had to use more ingenuity to stretch the tiny allocation of rice and find things we could add to the cooking pot – insects, birds, leaves and grasses, scraps the children managed to salvage from under the Japs' table.

That night, somehow I found room for Penny to sleep next to me in my hut. Space was already tight, but I prevailed upon my co-habitees to take pity on the child since she was completely alone. We were all crammed together, bodies touching, so that it was impossible to turn over, and sleep brought us no comfort other than a few hours of oblivion.

I woke that first night to the sound of Penny crying out. She was having a nightmare.

'It's all right, my darling,' I said, gathering her into my arms, knowing that of course it wasn't all right. 'It was only a dream. You're safe.'

That was when she told me that, night after night, she relived the horror of what she had gone through in the shipwreck.

'Mummy and I were blown into the sea. The ship was burning. It sank. We were in the water for ages. I thought we would drown. Then two nurses pulled us onto their life raft.' She began to cry. 'The sun was really hot and we had no water and no shade.'

'Sshh! Some of us are trying to sleep.' A voice from several feet away.

I took Penny's hand, leading her outside the hut. I needed to hear her story and I had a feeling she had had no opportunity to tell anyone until now.

We sat together on the ground, our backs against the

wooden wall of the hut, keeping our voices low so we didn't attract the attention of a passing guard.

'Tell me what happened, Penny.'

'The Japanese planes kept shooting at us in the sea. Mummy fell off the raft.'

I felt sick to the pit of my stomach. Penny should not have had to witness that.

'I don't think she was even hurt, but she was so weak and burnt by the sun and she went under the water. I was screaming and the nurses were trying to find her but she disappeared.'

I thought that was the end of the story but Penny continued.

'She floated up again. Away from us. We tried to paddle towards her, but the current was too strong.'

Penny bit her lip and I could see in the darkness that she was trembling.

'She got swept away. She was trying to reach us. Her hand was up in the air. Even though we couldn't see the rest of her. I kept screaming but we couldn't get to her. Then she wasn't there anymore.'

I pulled the little girl against me, cradling her in my arms. How was a child ever to get over such an experience? I was so angry I wanted to scream and shout and rail against the evil that had descended on our once safe and happy world.

I don't know how long we sat there, side-by-side, hand-in-hand, against the wooden hut wall, but we must have fallen asleep, as when I awoke, Penny was sleeping with her head in my lap. I stroked her hair. It felt rough and matted under my fingers, where once she had been crowned with hair as glossy and shiny as silk.

My thoughts drifted to Penny's mother, Rowena

Cameron. We had never been particular friends – she had been one of Veronica's acolytes – but we had been cordial neighbours. I had grown fond of Penny because of the benign neglect her parents had shown her. Completely absorbed in their own constant battling over Bertie's infidelities, they'd had little time for poor Penny. Rowena spent days in bed, the worse for drink after the binges she indulged in every time she and Bertie rowed. The gap in the hedge between their grand colonial house and our more modest dwelling was used regularly by Penny when she came to sit in our kitchen and eat the cakes my mother baked. It had always surprised me that the child had such a sunny disposition and a sense of mischief when she received so little attention at home.

I wondered why Bertie Cameron hadn't sent his wife and daughter out of Malaya before it was too late. Penny and Rowena could have been out of harm's way in Australia, as I presumed Evie and Jasmine were. As indeed we all should have been. But Bertie was the powerful and wealthy *tuan* of a shipping company and probably put his business interests ahead of his family's welfare. But perhaps that was too harsh a judgement to make. Bertie would have been no different from all the others who blithely assumed that a Japanese invasion – and a rapid British capitulation – was in the realms of fantasy. And poor Bertie was probably lying in a watery grave in the Malacca Straits.

PENNY'S APATHY CONTINUED, until gradually, as the weeks turned to months, she began to trust and eventually made friends among the other children in the camp. I kept her under my wing, giving her little tasks to do and encouraging her to participate in the improvised lessons that Sister Monica, one of the Dutch nuns, and I gave to the junior children. We had organised all the children into three age-based groupings and three other nuns supervised the smaller children, while two young teachers from one of the secondary schools in Singapore oversaw the teaching of the older ones. By rights, Penny should have been in the last group, but she was so fearful of losing sight of me that I let her stay in my class, where she was an invaluable help with the younger children.

Lessons were fraught with problems. For a start they were forbidden. Our prison guards banned any kind of education, as well as the use of paper, pencils and books. These exceptionally rare commodities were secreted and used extremely carefully. Even the oral teaching, which was the core of our methods, was not without danger. My mother was one of those who were appointed to keep watch and pass on a warning sign to us if the Japanese were near and likely to discover us. This was a task she took seriously – whenever she was well enough to perform it.

I had expected Veronica, as a friend of Rowena, to be pleased to see Penny and to show her kindness. But Veronica had never had time for children. Not until they were older – young adults like Cynthia. Even though Penny was the daughter of her friend, Veronica offered her no affection and barely acknowledged their connection. That was part of the enigma of Veronica that I will never understand. A woman who could move between great compassion and self-sacrifice through indifference to downright vindictiveness. And I had in my time experienced all of these from her.

9

BACK TO BANKA ISLAND

For the past few months we had been warned by our captors that we were now under risk from Allied air raids. To be frank, there were some of us who thought that friendly fire would be a fast, easy escape from the endless endurance of our life in camp.

By now there were no more regular deliveries of rice, and we were ordered to convert every available square foot of the camp into arable land to grow plants and root crops to keep us alive. The Japanese would take small parties of us into the jungle to forage for ferns, grasses and leaves. Any individual plots we had cultivated were now banned and had to be incorporated into the larger project of feeding the entire camp. This was a heavy blow to Marjorie, who had proved adept and green-fingered in turning vegetable scraps into new growth which she shared with Mum, and their friends Daphne and Beryl.

One morning, I was working at the back-breaking job of tilling the soil in preparation for the planting of sweet potatoes and tapioca roots.

'This is ridiculous.' The complainer was Mrs Van den

Bosch. 'The ground is baked hard. We've had no rain in weeks. It's like concrete.'

'Do shut up,' said Marjorie, testily. 'Even the Japs are digging now. It's do it or die.' Around their own dwellings, the guards had begun cultivating the land.

'What's the point of breaking up the soil when we have nothing to water it with?' The question from Beryl was a reasonable one, as all the wells were now almost dry, and we were down to a few inches of dirty water at the depths. We got the answer the following day.

'Get container for water. Everyone.' The instructions, relayed from the commandant via his translator, came at the end of a particularly long drawn out *tenko* in blistering heat.

We went around the camp searching for anything that could serve to carry water. On our return, more orders were barked at us to form groups of three and walk in file.

We were escorted by the guards about half a mile down a steep hill leading away from the camp, past the houses where the Japanese lived. At the bottom was a water hydrant, already surrounded by local Indonesian people. The Japanese guards enforced strict queuing in the rising morning heat. Around the pump was heavy mud where the water spilled from the hydrant and we had to tramp through it to fill our containers, the mud dragging on our feet, before trudging back up the steep and stony hill to the camp. There, we were ordered to water the crops we had planted.

'Excuse me?' a small voice piped up. It was Laura Hopkins. 'I wonder might we instead use the dirty water from the wells here on the crops and utilise this cleaner supply for drinking?'

'No! Do as say. Water on ground. Now.' The angry tone brooked no argument.

Eyes rolled. We had become accustomed to the illogical

near madness of our jailers and had lost the capacity or energy to get angry about it.

The following day, things got worse. After the interminable *tenko* – as usual protracted by the guards' evident lack of facility at simple maths, making even a basic counting exercise one that required endless repetition – Sergeant Shoei stepped forward.

He barked out orders and his translator repeated them. 'First water Japanese gardens. After fill Japanese baths. Then water crops here.' He pointed his stick at the plot we had dug.

A collective groan went up and I looked anxiously at Mum. She was only just recovering from a spell in the sick bay after a bad malaria attack and she was seriously debilitated. She intercepted my look and gave a little shake of her head to indicate I mustn't make a fuss on her behalf. Mum was not the only one who would find these additional trials overwhelming. The whole camp was getting weaker by the day.

After our exertions, absorbed with concern for Mum as Marjorie and I supported her back into the hut, I failed to notice the camp commandant as we passed him. The constant deterioration in the fortunes of Japan, under what even we in our closed environment knew to be the growing Allied advance, had made the Japanese even more petty and cruel towards us. We were supposed to be the shameful losers, and our persecutors did not want to lose sight of that. They now insisted we bow every time we happened to pass one of them as we went about our daily business. I had failed to do this and –crime of crimes – I had failed to do it to the highest-ranking man present. My punishment for this heinous misdemeanour was to stand hatless for an hour in

the midday sun, after my face was slapped so hard my lip
bled.

Another punishment often meted out was the spreading
of manure upon the crops. I was fortunate that it never
happened to me. The ordure in question was our own. The
hapless miscreants were expected to gather the waste from
the latrines in tin cans and spread our foul-smelling excre-
ment over the rows where we had planted sweet potatoes
and tapioca roots. The stench was indescribable – not just
for the spreaders but for the entire camp population. We
had descended to the lowest form of humiliation. It was also
a guaranteed way to spread disease more rapidly through
our already weak defences.

The misery of the worsening regime was alleviated for a
brief moment when we saw parcels with Red Cross labels
being unloaded from a lorry. We knew enough though not
to show our jubilance, as it might prove premature. There
was a delay of several days before the supplies were appor-
tioned out – the Japanese had first taken the lion's share of
the contents intended for us. Most of the medicines and
almost all the tinned foods were taken. They also pillaged
all the cigarettes and smoked them in front of us, throwing
the half-smoked butts to the ground for us to scrabble over
and divide up. Most of the chocolate was gone, leaving only
a small quantity on which the bloom of mould had
appeared, along with a tiny quantity of near-rancid cheese.
We divided it between us, but unlike the loaves and fishes,
all the minuscule portions did was make our normally
dormant taste buds long for more, without in any way sating
our hunger.

It was not long after the Red Cross delivery that Mum
took ill again. By now my once roly-poly mother was a tiny,
skeletal creature, barely able to muster the strength to

speak. Suffering from another of her recurrent malaria attacks, she was showing the signs of it developing into dengue fever. Her body was covered with an itchy red rash; she developed a raging fever and complained of blinding headaches. Her gums were bleeding badly, and she was vomiting frequently – often with blood. In normal circumstances, rest and plenty of water would have seen her recover, but these were far from normal circumstances. Severe malnutrition and the lack of clean water were making her so weak her body had little or no resistance to fight the disease.

Mum's friend Marjorie had swollen from her legs and ankles to the middle of her torso, giving her the strange lopsided appearance of a woman who was hugely obese in her lower half with an emaciated upper body.

'What's the matter with Marjorie?' I asked the nursing sister who was caring for Marjorie and Mum. 'Why is she ballooning up like that?'

The nurse gave me a sad look. 'Beriberi. It's caused by severe vitamin deficiency and there's no way to reverse it without high doses of Vitamin B.'

She didn't need to tell me there was none.

'What will happen to her?' I was speaking in a hushed voice. I didn't want either Mum or Marjorie to hear. While I was no fan of Marjorie, I knew how fond Mum was of her.

The nurse, Sister Becky, one of the Australians, stretched her mouth into a thin line and said, 'You want the hard facts?'

I nodded, although I could tell I wasn't going to find what she had to say easy.

'There are two forms of beriberi – dry and wet. With the dry version the body shrivels up and seems to be shrinking until eventually the organs collapse. With the wet, it causes a weak heart and poor circulation and the body's tissues fill with oedema until the whole system fails. Basically, you drown in your own poisonous fluid.' She gave me a sad smile. 'It's not a pretty ending, Mary.'

I felt desperately sorry for Marjorie. At times she had been irritating and strident, but she had been a good and faithful friend to Mum and if she were to die, it would devastate Mum.

'And my mother?'

'I hope she'll get over the dengue, but you have to understand, Mary, that every time she gets sick her body gets weaker and her resistance and capacity to fight reduce too. Your mum is badly undernourished, and her heart is under a lot of strain.' She sucked her lips inwards. 'Look, I'm going to be honest with you. Unless our circumstances change radically, I doubt your mother will be strong enough to last another bout of this type of sickness. She's just too frail.'

I had let Mum down. I wanted to help her to get through this terrible time and return to Dad when it was over. With Sister Becky's words I knew that was now highly improbable.

My visits to Mum's bedside were as often and as long as allowed – which was not very much – the nurses were very strict. I held her hand and tried to keep her cool whenever her fever raged. She was in a lot of pain with the headaches and I sensed she was giving up the struggle. At night I lay awake, weeping silent tears that Mum's life was ending in such a miserable manner.

There was little time left for her.

When I thought it couldn't possibly get any worse, it did.

IF WE HAD BELIEVED that the men's camp would be our final place of imprisonment until the day we hoped to be liberated, we were to be proved wrong. And we did all believe it, so it came as a terrible shock when we were told that we were to be moved again just over a year after we arrived in the men's camp.

The increased level of cruelty on the part of our oppressors, the further diminishing rations and the growing number of rumours, fuelled our hope and belief that the war must be drawing to a close and an Allied victory was in sight. Being told we were to be transferred to another place filled us with terror. It could well mean that the Japanese wished to hide us away in some remote area where we might never be found should an Allied victory come. Or worse still, they would take us deep into the jungle and execute us.

We were divided into groups to make the journey separately. I was worried I would be separated from my ailing mother but thanks to Veronica, who swapped with me, I was in the group who would accompany the occupants of the hospital hut and their nurses. We were to be the last of four groups to leave.

After travelling by truck – distressing enough for seriously ill and dying patients – we carried the stretcher-bound patients onto the deck of an old tanker boat. There were no sanitary arrangements on board and the only way anyone could use the lavatory was by passing around a single rice bowl donated by one of the nurses to serve as an inadequate chamber pot among about a hundred of us.

As soon as we moved out into the strait, the ship was caught up in a tropical storm that sent the ancient boat bucking and groaning, filling us with terror and causing many to be violently sick. I lay on the deck, pelted by driving rain and washed by waves, clutching Mum's hand, convinced that she was going to die while we were still at sea. All around us sick women and children were vomiting and crying out, distressed and terrified as thunder and lightning split the sky. The boat rose rapidly on the swell, then plummeted vertically downwards from the crest of the waves and we all feared for our lives.

Not long after the storm subsided, someone pointed through the thick mist to the long finger of a seemingly endless and all-too familiar pier, appearing in front of the ship. There was a collective intake of breath. We were going back to Banka Island, and that must mean to the miserable Muntok camp where our nightmare had begun. I felt my throat close. Next to me one of the Australian nurses let out a groan that spoke for us all.

Mum was now unconscious. Marjorie was in a worse state, lying next to her, under a filthy sheet, the elephantine swelling of her lower limbs evident through the thin cotton cover. Yet both those brave women survived the rest of our journey – the last part of it mercifully short.

Instead of that long terrible march through the jungle with heavy luggage, we were herded onto a truck and driven to our destination. When we arrived, to everyone's initial relief, the Muntok Camp we were taken to was not the one where we had started out. The wooden huts were new and looked more like those of a native village. And the whole place looked clean. There were half a dozen large concrete-floored sleeping huts furnished with newly woven mats to sleep on in significantly more space than we had been used to. To cap it all, there were three designated kitchen areas and a large supply of chopped firewood.

I turned to Veronica, who had been there for two days already. 'This seems a big improvement.' I felt a surge of hope that Nurse Becky's statement about our needing a reversal of circumstances might prove prophetic.

'Don't speak too soon, Mary. You haven't seen the toilets yet.'

Veronica led me around to the latrines and to my dismay I saw they consisted only of an open pit with bamboo slats over the top.

She pulled a face. 'One is expected to squat with one foot on each slat. Better hope your balance is up to it, as there's nothing between you and the pit.'

The first time I used the facilities I was filled with bowel-paralysing horror. Between the wooden slats I could see a seething mass of maggots. To add insult to injury, the latrines were sited immediately adjacent to the kitchens, making the task of preparing our miserable rations even more onerous and noxious.

However, that first night there was more food than we had been accustomed to – including some fish. A number of inmates overindulged and were sick as a consequence. I was not one of them, my hunger tempered by guilt and anxiety over Mum.

While the plentiful food that first night was good news, the bad news was we had no water to wash and were forced to retire to bed filthy after our exhausting journey.

The quantity and variety of food did not continue either. Within a week, all nine water wells in the camp, overwhelmed by the inflow of people, were dry. We were back to another daily trudge up and down a treacherously muddy hill to reach a stream, half a mile away.

One of the bitter ironies of our lengthy imprisonment was that the more beautiful our surroundings, the greater our torment. Here at Muntok, women increasingly fell victim to disease. Marjorie was not the only one with beriberi, and both the wet and dry variants were now frequent throughout the camp. Mrs Hopkins and Beryl both had the dry version and while still able to stand they now moved around the camp like a pair of staggering drunks, unsteady on their shrivelled feet and legs.

Veronica came upon me that night as I was getting ready for bed. She told me she was going to try and get some quinine for Mum.

'How?' I had noticed that Veronica's services to Sergeant Shoei appeared to have ceased since we'd arrived in Muntok. 'I thought Shoei–'

'Had stopped screwing me?'

I was shocked by the crudeness of her language but didn't want to give her the satisfaction of seeing that. 'Yes.'

'There comes a point when even the Japs would rather do without, than do the dirty with us. Can't say I blame them.' She gave her little tinkling laugh. 'It must be like having intercourse with a bag of spanners. Except spanners don't smell and have sores all over them.' She spoke without bitterness, amused rather than angry at the state we were all now in. 'No. I have an idea how I can get to the supplies though.'

'How?'

'Better you don't know.' She gave me a tight little smile. 'No promises, but I'll do my best.'

Veronica was as good as her word and the aspirin she managed to obtain meant Mum's inevitable passage to death was at least without the levels of pain she would otherwise have had to endure.

Mum died in the middle of the afternoon of what our collective tallying of the dates indicated was December 18th 1944. I was with her, holding her hand as she slipped away. She'd been unconscious for most of that last day, but I am certain she knew I was there. Just before she died, she opened her eyes, looked at me and said, 'Sorry, Mary. I must go now. Your father's waiting for me.' Her eyes closed and she breathed her last breath.

It was only after the war was over and I finally received word that Dad too was gone, that I discovered he had died just a few days before her, on December 15th.

Mum's was not the only mortality that day. As well as beriberi, the camp's death toll was added to by the spread of something we called Banka Fever. This was a form of cerebral malaria and every bed in the hospital hut was filled with cases. The nurses were seriously handicapped in their heroic efforts to help the sick by the absence of medication and medical equipment. The Japanese had the supplies, but continued to withhold them, offering a completely inadequate token amount of quinine each month, implying it was more than we deserved. By the time the year drew to its miserable close, around fifteen women were laid to rest in the jungle clearing where Mum was buried.

I had to dig my own mother's grave. This is not something I ever expected to have to do. Before we laid her to rest, I slipped Dad's letter under her hands. She had treasured it all through our captivity, reading it every night before she went to sleep. Now it was falling apart, water-stained, torn and so fragile I doubted I'd have been able to read it even if I'd wanted to.

Veronica made a simple cross and, using a nail heated in the cooking fire, burnt Mum's name and the date onto it. I knew it wouldn't stand long over the little patch of jungle where we buried her. The jungle would take over and eradicate any signs of the growing number of graves there. Marjorie, now in the final stages of beriberi, that would result in her joining Mum in that little corner of the island in just a matter of weeks, was unable to attend Mum's funeral.

One of the camp's small number of missionaries presided over the prayers. Penny had by now joined the choir and she and the other members gathered in the clearing and sang a hymn Mum had liked in church back in George Town, *Lord of All Hopefulness*. Yet on the day we buried her I had never felt so without hope.

I stared at that pathetic little wooden cross with only her name burnt onto it: Janet Mary Helston. A tear trickled down my cheek. I brushed it away. No time for crying. I had latrines to empty before the evening meal.

CHRISTMAS THAT YEAR was just another day. Previously, we had tried to make an effort to sing, to put on little shows or watch the children entertaining us with a nativity play. But the Christmas of 1944, as the war was going the way of the Allies, an end to our torment seemed further from our reach than at any other time since we'd entered captivity. No news of the world outside reached us and we were nearing the point where we could no longer imagine any way out of our suffering than death.

10

THE LAST CAMP

W e were to remain at Muntok for less than six months. Yet again, we were moved at the whim of the Japanese. This was the worst wrench of all. I would be making a move for the first time without Mum, forced to abandon that little patch of Banka where her body lay. The dense jungle would reclaim the ground in which she was buried and there would be no remaining sign of the passing of my poor brave mother. Not for her a quiet, well-tended plot in the graveyard in George Town, with my father laid beside her and a stone headstone with an inscription.

If I had ever thought of my parents' last resting place, it was that it would be far ahead in the future. Maybe twenty or thirty years away. Mum's grave being lost forever in the dense jungle of Banka Island would never have entered my wildest dreams. I had to take consolation from the fact that she was not alone there but surrounded by the graves of many of our friends – almost eighty of them by the time we left the island. There was a large complement from our dormitory in the Van den Boschs' house –

Mum's friends Beryl and Marjorie, the young bride Sharon Henderson, Mrs Hopkins, Mrs Van den Bosch and her small daughter.

I was far from hale and hearty myself. Like all of us, I had not been exempt from attacks of dysentery and malaria, but I was younger and fitter than many of the women. As we moved into the first months of 1945, dying was more likely than staying alive for anyone who became ill.

Everyone in our sisterhood looked up to the Australian nurses. To us mere mortals, they were indestructible and optimistic forces of nature. Yet, as 1945 advanced, they too began to succumb to the tentacles of death. Dying should have become banal, yet each one was a personal tragedy and a source of grief and loss to us. They were all individuals. Each death carried with it a remembered kindness, a regretted angry word, a joint punishment or a shared joke. The women who had irritated or annoyed us at the beginning of our terrible journey, such as Marjorie or Mrs Van den Bosch, had become essential members of our close-knit sorority and we mourned their passing.

I marvel that any of us did survive, when we had so many examples around us of others falling by the wayside. What right did we have to live, when our companions had so easily slipped away into death? It is a question I am still asking and probably always will.

It was Veronica who was most responsible for keeping me going in those last days on Banka Island. She made it her mission to keep me alive. When I reached the depths of despair, hopelessness and complete physical exhaustion, I had an overwhelming desire to just lie down and give up. Death was an inevitability. Staying alive was a deliberate choice and certainly not the easiest one. Every time I was at the point of collapse as we slithered our way up the mud path from the stream, Veronica was there behind me, telling me to keep moving.

'Think of the kid,' she would say. 'The Cameron girl depends on you. If you give up, she'll be dead in a week.'

She was right. Penny needed me. Maybe not for her physical survival, but for the love and affection which made that survival possible. I was all she had. If I were to die, as her parents had, who would remain for her with any connection to her old life? And, in turn, Penny was all I had. I couldn't have loved her more if she were my own daughter. She was my motivation to go on, but it was Veronica who consistently reminded me of that fact.

OUR LAST JOURNEY proved to be the worst so far. All we were informed was that, like yo-yos, we were heading back to the main island of Sumatra.

Veronica and Penny were among those who left in the first detachment. Everyone in that group survived the horrors of a journey that took over thirty-six hours.

I was included among the second group, ordered to leave at dawn the following morning. This party included the sick and dying women and their nurses. Those of us on our feet were required to act as stretcher bearers.

'Some of these patients can't be moved.' One of the nursing sisters spoke out, addressing her objections to the camp commandant himself. 'These women are close to death. It's a matter of hours. It would be an act of supreme cruelty to move them. Can't we wait with the worst cases and just move those we believe can withstand the journey?'

She was rewarded with a fierce slap across the face. The blow was so hard that it sent her reeling backwards.

So, we left the camp, and were taken on open trucks back to that long endless jetty we had trudged along so many times before. The skies opened up in a torrential rainstorm. One of the patients was already dead.

Sergeant Shoei oversaw our next task. All of us capable of standing were ordered to unload the household goods of the Japanese from waiting trucks, pile them onto handcarts and drag those carts the length of that interminable pier to the waiting boat.

Laura Hopkins was beside me. She and I had become close since we had each suffered the loss of our mothers. Like me, she was an only child and knew nothing of the whereabouts of her father.

'There's not going to be room for us on that boat once all this is stowed,' she said, her mouth set in a grim line.

'I know,' I replied. 'Do you think they'll make us wait here on the jetty for another boat?'

She closed her eyes. Neither of us needed to voice what we were each feeling, that our numbers were going to be seriously depleted by the time we got to Sumatra.

It turned out to be worse than the long wait we'd dreaded. Once the boat was loaded, we were ordered back onto the trucks, now with several of the patients dead, and driven back to the camp we had left that morning. There we buried the dead and the following day set off again for that long pier that symbolised the endless, hopeless nature of our captivity and the growing likelihood that we would not survive the rest of the war.

Our final walk along that wooden pier was like the journey to Calvary. The heavy cross we had to bear was the carrying of stretchers, until at last we had loaded all the sick and dying patients onto the deck. Anyone capable of walking, no matter how weak, was expected to do so and I will never forget the pathetic sight of women with dry beriberi, Mum's third Penang friend, Daphne, among them, shuffling along, emaciated legs splaying outwards under them, so that they had the gait of the heavily intoxicated. Those with the other form dragged their inflated bodies on swollen feet, a slow-moving procession of women who resembled the Michelin Man in the French rubber tyre advertisements.

On board, the stretcher cases were laid side-by-side on deck, with no protection from the fiery heat of the midday sun. The only conclusion we could draw was that the Japs wanted our numbers to be significantly diminished by the time we reached our destination.

The rest of us were loaded into the hold with the rats and the filthy rice sacks, and the hatches closed on us. Inside, it was pitch dark, hot as an oven and with no ventilation. We sat crammed together, praying that the passage would be fast and calm and that our ordeal would soon be over.

But day turned to night and while it became mercifully cooler for us in our sealed furnace, those on deck endured the cold with no cover to ease the shock of the changed temperature on their sun-blackened, blistered bodies.

Inevitably, after landing, we gathered on the dockside to go through *tenko*. This was repeated several times – in the full glare of the sun – until some bright spark worked out that the reason the numbers didn't add up was that the Japs had failed to include the dead in their count.

The worst part of the journey was still to come. We waited in the heat all day beside the railway track, until eventually a train appeared. The impatience of the Japanese boiled over into anger. I suppose that their role as the guardians of a company of half-dead women was not a glorious one. They must also have been on short rations themselves – there were severe food shortages everywhere as the Allies tightened the net, blocking shipping and supplies. But this was neither clear nor significant to us then. We had become zombie-like, victims of our oppressors' voodoo, so that we no longer searched for optimistic signs, or indeed felt any emotions – just a passive numbness and a longing for it all to be over – even if that meant death.

As the guards screamed, exhorting us to move faster, we carried the stretcher cases into the goods vans and laid them on a floor that was black with a heavy layer of coal dust.

Our own accommodation was no more salubrious. All of us, including those among the seriously ill who were able to move, were herded into filthy carriages which had also been used to haul coal and were thick with the evidence. We were given just one small can of water – not enough to drink, but just sufficient to dampen a cloth with which to ease the fever that so many of us were experiencing.

By the morning, half a dozen more women had died. The heat in the carriages was stifling, the air barely breathable. Several dysentery cases made the confinement more hellish. There were no toilet facilities, no openable windows, so that their soil had to be collected in a can and poured out of a small hatch near the ceiling.

As night fell, the train came to a halt with a screech of brakes and we gave a collective sigh of relief that it was over.

It wasn't.

We were held all night on that crowded stationary train, tightly packed like candles in a box, rigid, unable to move our limbs to stretch. Our only sustenance was a bit of brown bread, gritty, hard as a rock, and no water.

At daybreak, as the light filtered through the grimy windows, I watched Sergeant Shoei strut along the platform past our carriage.

One of the guards flung open the door. '*Tenko!*' he screamed.

AFTER A LONG DRIVE into the dense core of the Sumatran interior, we arrived at an abandoned rubber estate. If my suspicion that the Japanese wanted to hide us away until we died was right, they could not have chosen a better place. As we clambered down from the trucks, our numbers significantly diminished, I turned to Laura. 'No one will ever find us here.'

She looked at me, her face expressionless. 'Do you think we'll be executed?'

'I doubt it. Why bother when we're all dying anyway? They could have killed the lot of us when they first captured us. That would have freed up all those guards for active duty and saved the pitiful amount they spent on feeding us. Why do it now, when it isn't going to make any difference?' I tried to swallow the bitterness in my voice, but I couldn't. 'Besides, they take sadistic pleasure in seeing us suffer.'

'You're probably right.' She offered a weak smile.

The Dutch planters who ran this rubber estate had followed the prescribed 'scorched earth' policy before they left. The metal tanks once used to hold the liquid rubber, the rolling machines to press it into sheets, the smoke house, the storage sheds – all were destroyed and the crushed and burnt remains heaped on the ground in rusting piles. Only the coolies' huts remained and, after more than three years of abandonment, the tin roofs were leaking, creating puddles of mud and rainwater on the floors.

I went to claim my sleeping spot, which Penny had reserved for me. She was relieved to see me and pressed her thin body to mine, clinging like a limpet to a rock.

'Don't leave me again, Miss Helston,' was all she managed to say.

I went to reclaim my paltry belongings, which had been transported along with the more substantial quantities of the Japanese goods, only to find they had been looted en route.

All around me anguished cries went up, as other women discovered which of their possessions had been pilfered. Among the missing items was my mother's mother-of-pearl vanity case, in which she kept her nail scissors, a metal nail file, a tortoiseshell comb and a photograph of my father. It had been all I had left of her. Most of her other possessions, like mine, had been bartered away over the years for a few mouldy vegetables or a scrap of meat to add to the pot. Of my own belongings, the only other dress I possessed was gone, as well as the threadbare towel that had represented my last vestige of dignity. But the most terrible, soul-sapping loss was my engagement ring. I hadn't had it on my person when travelling as that was too risky – the Japs often searched us for any remaining jewellery. Instead, I'd hidden it in a pouch sewn into the lining at the bottom of my battered canvas holdall. It was the only thing I had been determined never to be parted from. Even when my body screamed out with hunger, I had resisted the urge to barter it for food. I'd told myself that the hunger would inevitably return, but once the ring was gone, it was lost forever. That ring was all I had of Frank. It was everything to me. I stared, disbelieving and bereft at where the lining of my bag was slashed apart with a knife.

I collapsed to my knees and wept.

Penny came and sat beside me, cradling me as I sobbed, just as I had comforted her when she first came to the camp.

'Come on, Miss Helston. Your boyfriend would have

wanted you to be brave. And tears won't bring it back, will they?'

She was right. I channelled my grief into anger. But it was such a waste. More than three years of guarding that ring with my life, only for it to be stolen. I might as well have bartered it for food. Drying my eyes with the back of my hand, I stumbled onto my feet.

'Are you going to show me the sights, Penny? What's the new hotel like?' I gave her a feeble grin and she smiled back. Her bravery and positive attitude made me feel ashamed.

As Penny led me around our new home, she told me the bad news. 'There are no toilets and no running water.'

I looked at her in disbelief. 'Nothing at all?'

She shook her head. 'We have to wash in the stream where the Japs can see us.' She looked mortified. 'And as their huts are upstream, the water's dirty by the time we get our turn. It's horrible and they watch us while we're bathing.' She fixed me with her big sad eyes. 'They sit on the bank and laugh at us because we're so thin and ugly.'

I pulled her towards me and held her emaciated body against mine. I'd gladly die myself if I could somehow get Penny out of here alive and give her a chance to finish what was left of her childhood and experience a very different life.

With God again showing a cruel sense of humour, though life on the Sumatran rubber estate was to prove harsher than anywhere we had stayed before, the property was a place of great natural beauty.

The area immediately around the huts was dark and oppressive, overshadowed by the tall bulk of the rubber trees, which formed a dense canopy to shut out any light. Yet, the little stream – a source of pollution and infection –

had an innocent beauty that belied the poisons we absorbed from it.

The flowers that surrounded us splashed vivid colours like an impressionist painting over the dark green of the encroaching jungle. Brilliantly hued butterflies and colourful dragonflies danced over the deceptively clear waters of the stream. Even the forest ferns were things of beauty. Rather than dull matte greens, they offered up a myriad of shades from deepest green to a shimmering blue. Their leaves were equally varied, from broad and straight to the delicate tracery of a paper doily at a tea party. Some were grouped into the shapes of spearheads while others curved into domes like umbrellas.

The cicadas offered a background hissing noise upon which birds of all varieties overlaid their songs. Plaintive calls, delicate trills, love songs, soft whistles, insistent warbles. And the plumage! The hornbill, its red, orange and yellow head with enlarged curved bill contrasting a simple and elegant black body – like a lady in a little black dress wearing too much make-up and an over-elaborate head-dress. Birds with yellow stomachs, parrots, woodpeckers, birds of paradise and vibrant kingfishers.

Not a day passed when I didn't long for a sketch book and pencils. I was no great artist, but I'd always enjoyed sketching and here, where there was so much to inspire me, I had no means to indulge – short of scratching in the ground with twigs.

Against this brightness and beauty, we lived out our days in disease, starvation, misery, pain and exhaustion. Not a single woman or child was exempt from the illness our conditions forced upon us. A small scratch from a thorn or a bite from an insect could transform into agonising tropical ulcers for which we had no antidote and could treat only by applying a smear of palm oil and tying a piece of rag over the top. Beriberi was endemic throughout the camp and the polluted river added to our ills.

We were so weak and undernourished that the only time we had the strength to chop firewood and dig graves was in the early morning. Grave-digging was no longer an occasional activity, but part of our daily rota of tasks, like scavenging for forest grasses, lighting the cooking fires and preparing our meagre meals.

THE FIRST TIME we saw Allied airplanes overhead we all felt a surge of joy. We had no idea that peace had already been declared in Europe. But time wore on and still there was no end in sight for us, and with the death toll mounting, we all grew more and more dispirited and fell into a kind of passive state where nothing touched us anymore.

It was then that I fell dangerously ill. I wasn't even aware of it, such was my condition. I have no memory of those days, other than a vague awareness of the nurses and the blurred faces of others – Veronica included. It was malaria and the only quinine we had was what we obtained from boiling cinchona tree bark. This was unrefined and not strong enough to treat advanced forms of malaria and I was fading fast. I was unaware of it, but Penny was sick too. She was in the bed next to mine, critically ill.

That's when Veronica took it upon herself to steal medical supplies from the Japanese.

I have no idea how she did it, but she managed to get into their stores and steal a box of quinine and some bottles of antiseptic. If she hadn't done this, Penny and I – and several others – would have died.

We made a recovery and though still extremely weak, were able to leave the care of the nurses.

As Veronica must have known was inevitable, the Japs eventually realised that medicines had been stolen from the storeroom where they hoarded them. They took three women randomly from the camp and said they would be punished until the culprit owned up.

One of those women was me. Another was Laura and the third was one of the Australian nurses.

We were tied to posts in the area that was once the *padang* of the rubber estate, where the daily roll calls would have taken place and where we were summoned every day for *tenko*.

The sun was savage, and we had no head coverings. The hut leaders asked the Japanese if they might offer us theirs. The request was denied. Sergeant Shoei approached us with a heavy wooden stick.

Of course, I had endured many beatings, countless face slaps, had my legs struck with rifle butts and even been punched in the face. But now, still weak from my sickness, starving, dispirited and barely able to stand, I knew I could not survive what was about to happen.

Writing this is incredibly hard. I don't want to remember the feelings that went through me. I wanted to get it over with, above all else. Death was inevitable, so all I wanted was for it to come quickly. But I was also afraid. Filled with abject terror at the pain I would have to endure before oblivion came to me. The worst part was waiting for that first blow to land. I lifted up my eyes to the sky and closed them, telling myself that soon I would be with Mum again and reunited with Frank.

Sergeant Shoei was pacing up and down screaming. His

custom was for his corporal to do the dirty work – he preferred to watch from the sidelines.

Shoei directed his anger into the lineup of women facing us. I suddenly realised he knew who was responsible.

'Someone will die here. I promise you this.'

He moved towards me and landed a blow from his stick across my shoulders. The pain was an electric bolt through my entire body. My knees buckled, but the rope holding me to the post kept me in place, burning into my paper-thin skin.

Shoei let forth an angry burst which his translator reiterated in his stilted English. 'They die, one then other, until person who stole confess crime.'

He swung the stick again. This time it was lower and crashed into my arm above the elbow. I heard the crack as the bone snapped. For a few moments I felt nothing. Then the burning, stabbing agony began and I cried out.

That's when Veronica stepped forward.

She walked straight up to Shoei until she was so close, they were practically touching. Looking up into his face, she said, 'Enough. You know damn well it was me. Stop this game. Let them go. They did nothing. It was me.'

There was a collective gasp around the camp. For her bravery was twofold – in stealing the medicines in the first place, then in admitting it when she knew it meant certain death.

For Sergeant Shoei it must have been a huge loss of face. He may have no longer been having sexual relations with Veronica, but there must have been some residual feelings. Shoei, who was a brute to the rest of us, had always been lighter on her.

But Hell hath no fury like a Japanese officer scorned. Veronica would suffer for his loss of face.

They locked her inside a bamboo cage, deprived of food and water, in the full heat of the sun. She was there all day and all night until they took her away to torture her. I don't know what they did but their favoured methods were to tie people up with hands behind their backs and suspend them from a rope until their shoulders dislocated, or cover their faces with sacks and pour water into their throats. These punishments had been meted out to a Dutch 'free' woman they had accused of spying, back in our time in the houses.

After three days, in which we had no idea whether Veronica was alive or dead, they brought her out to the *padang* at *tenko*. We assumed her punishment was done and she was about to be allowed to rejoin us. Instead, they made us stand in a circle while they stripped her naked.

Veronica showed no fear, even though she was barely able to stand, and her dislocated arms hung uselessly at her sides. She was slumped forward, her legs barely able to support her, her head raised to look up at the sky, no sign of self-pity on her face. It was a stinking-hot day and we could see the perspiration heavy on her skin – although we tried not to stare at her, to make her public humiliation worse. Instead we looked at the baked hard ground under our feet and tried to pretend this was the same as every other *tenko*. Yet each one of us knew that it wasn't. A chill crept over me in spite of the burning sun.

Sergeant Shoei screamed an order to his men and they began to beat Veronica savagely with heavy wooden batons, knocking her off her feet and continuing to club her where she was sprawled on the ground. The beating lasted until we could hardly see her skin under the thick film of blood.

Veronica never cried out. Not once.

Sergeant Shoei screamed at us all. 'This what happen when steal from us. This woman bad. This woman thief.' He paced up and down, fixing his eyes on each of us and avoiding looking at her. 'Steal from us is steal from Emperor. If steal from us, you die.'

They tied Veronica to a post in the middle of the *padang* under the searing heat of the sun, with no shade, food or water.

None of us could do anything for her, so we stood in a circle, waiting with her, waiting for her to die. No one could possibly survive what had happened in front of us, let alone what had happened away from our eyes. Her body was broken. The pain must have been indescribable. Standing with her was all we could offer. Our useless, helpless presence. Our bearing witness to her fate.

After losing consciousness for a while, Veronica opened her swollen eyes and lifted her head high and began to sing. A frail, tuneless voice, barely above a whisper.

We began to sing with her. We packed up our troubles in our old kit bags, with cockles and mussels, and did the Lambeth Walk on the long road to Tipperary.

Veronica must have known what would happen and that it would be the fastest way to bring her suffering to an end. The singing was a deliberate provocation. The Japs went insane.

Sergeant Shoei, after the beating, had absented himself, shutting himself away in his office in a wooden hut on the other side of the *padang*. Perhaps he couldn't bear to see her like that. But as his men began screaming and shouting at us all to shut up, Shoei came striding out, yelled at Veronica to shut up and when she didn't, he took out his pistol and fired a bullet through her head.

Veronica died instantly, her head sagging forward over her thin little neck.

As that single gunshot rang out across the camp, a huge

flock of birds flew up from the adjacent trees and we all stood, our heads lowered, relieved that it was over for Veronica, but horrified by the brutal atrocity we had witnessed. We stood in silence until someone started to say The Lord's Prayer and everyone joined in.

We buried Veronica that afternoon. With my broken arm, which the nurses had bound for me, I was not able to do much to help. The women wrapped her in the threadbare sheet from her bed and carried her across the *padang* into the jungle to the area where all our dead were interred. They dug a grave for her, and as Veronica had done for Mum, one of the nuns made a cross from a couple of branches and scratched her name on it. Veronica Leighton.

She died on August 9th. We didn't know, but it was the day of the bombing of Nagasaki, following that of Hiroshima, three days earlier. But Sergeant Shoei must have known. Perhaps that, and the knowledge that a Japanese surrender would soon be inevitable, had inflamed his anger. At any other time, Veronica's transgressions might have incurred only a beating. But we knew none of this.

After we buried Veronica, I noticed that Cynthia Pickering, Veronica's adoring acolyte, the Eurasian sister of Cyril, was weeping copiously.

'It's my fault that Veronica's dead.'

She was sobbing convulsively, so it was hard to make out what she was saying.

'Why do you say it's your fault, Cynthia? Veronica died because she was stealing medicine. She was an incredibly brave woman and we should all be grateful for her sacrifice, but it's not your fault. Almost every one of us has benefited at some time from what Veronica did.'

Cynthia herself had benefited from the morphine Veronica had obtained when the young woman had had an abscess under her tooth. One of the nurses had extracted it in the most painful and primitive manner and, without the morphine, I doubt Cynthia would have been able to bear the excruciating pain.

'Not because of the medicines.' Her voice was soft, barely more than a whisper. 'Back in the houses, the deputy commandant picked me out. Sergeant Shoei chose me to be his comfort lady. I was only fifteen. I'm a virgin. Veronica stepped in and took my place.' Cynthia's face was streaked with tears. 'If I had gone with him, Veronica wouldn't have had to. He wouldn't have been so angry with her. She'd still be alive.'

'I don't understand. How did she do that if he'd already chosen you?' I found it hard to believe that Shoei would have been anything other than obdurate if challenged.

Under the sheen of tears, I could see she was blushing. 'He was grabbing hold of me and Miss Veronica started to speak to him. She said things. Told him the things she would do for him. She said he was a powerful man and needed a skilled woman not a girl. She flattered him and she bragged about all the things she could do for him.' She brushed away her tears with the back of her hand. 'After what she said to him, he wasn't interested in me anymore.'

I sighed. A long heavy sigh. I remembered Veronica telling me how she used men's attraction to get her own ends. It was now evident it wasn't just her own ends, but to protect and support others.

The longer I had known Veronica Leighton, the more I came to recognise what a complex woman she was. It would be tempting to say that I had misjudged the old Veronica, the woman who stole other women's men, who used her cruel tongue to belittle others, but that wouldn't be true. Veronica was all those things and more.

What she did and said to others in Penang before the war can only be condemned – yet it can also be explained. Her background before her marriage was shrouded in mystery. Her fits of black depressive moods drained her and embittered her. Her empty, meaningless, sexual liaisons provided her with a form of validation in the short term, but they consumed her with self-loathing in the long.

It was war that gave Veronica a sense of purpose and an outlet for her courage and her administrative and organisational skills.

I tried to comfort Cynthia and I hope I managed to reassure her that she was blameless in our friend's death.

But with Veronica's passing I found it much harder myself to exist in captivity. Much harder to sustain my spirits and my will to survive.

We had absolutely no idea our ordeal would soon be ending. We had no communication with the outside world. No radio. No newspaper. And the Japanese continued to act as our invincible masters. And on our part, we had given up the fight. Veronica's savage death had shattered the last vestiges of hope among us and a dangerous and deep-rooted apathy took over the entire camp.

LIBERATION CAME LATE TO US. A full week after the signing of Japan's unconditional surrender on September 2nd and more than a month after the atomic bombing of Hiroshima. No one knew where we were.

I understand now how perilous our situation was and how lucky we were not to have all been killed in those days between the atomic bombing and the surrender. The Allied forces had no idea where the numerous internment camps were, particularly on Sumatra. Once the atomic bomb, with its terrible unleashing of mass destruction, had fallen on Hiroshima and Nagasaki, we would have been at critical risk that our captors could have exacted revenge upon us and executed us all.

I know now there were plans to do this, but it is a sign of the collapse of discipline and communication in the Japanese army, rather than the compassion of any individual commandants, that these orders were not fulfilled. Our captors were as apathetic and demoralised as we were.

In truth, we were expendable – not only by the Japanese, but also by the Allies. If a few thousand civilian women and children should happen to be executed by the Japanese in reprisals, before the Allied armies could get to us and make us safe, so be it. We were as inconsequential as dandelion clocks blowing in a breeze.

The bitter irony was that the number of fatalities increased the nearer we got to our eventual liberation. I often wonder now if, in those dreadful last days, we had known that freedom was just around the corner, whether some of those who died might have marshalled the strength to survive? But we had been through too many false dawns to sustain hope.

The day we were liberated from the camp, Sergeant Shoei shot himself. As the armoured cars and lorries burst through the gates, he went into his quarters, put his revolver to his head and blew his brains out. A much faster death than the one he had afforded Veronica. I am not ashamed to say I cursed him even in his death.

The camp commandant and the rest of the guards lined up, heads hanging, like stray dogs, surrendering to our Australian army liberators. I saw the fear in the guards' eyes, the desperation for it all to be over so they could go home and get on with their lives. Some of them were virtually boys, little tinpot warriors, playing at soldiers in their green khaki uniforms with the gold stars on their caps and their no-longer-highly-polished knee boots.

Sergeant Shoei hadn't been a boy though. He must have been in his late forties. I am absolutely certain that he killed himself because in the end he felt ashamed. Veronica had shamed him. Her bravery. His barbarity.

I know more than I care to about men who take their own lives, having come up against suicide twice. Oddly, both of them killed themselves because of Veronica Leighton. Ralph out of despair when Veronica left him. He had lost her, lost me, lost his future and his will to live. He knew he had messed everything up. But there was no despair in Sergeant Shoei. His death was an act of pure cowardice, a refusal to accept responsibility for his role in the war, for his running of the camp, for the savage treatment of us all, for the needless deaths from starvation and disease, for the medicines he kept locked away and refused to have dispensed. Maybe he didn't feel able to return to his wife and children, knowing the things that he had done and that had been done in the name of his emperor. Surrender too was probably too great a shame for him – subjugating himself to the enemy he had been trained to despise. So, he died like the coward he was.

As I was driven out of the camp for the last time, I thought of all the brave women I had known during our captivity, those who had died prematurely and needlessly. My mother – a woman in her fifties, fit and healthy when we were captured, crushed and broken by hunger, exhaustion and disease. Her friends Beryl, Marjorie and Daphne, stalwarts of colonial Penang, formidable ladies, pillars of the bridge club and the church choir. Poor Sharon Henderson, captured a week after her marriage and now dead.

It turned out that the men from whom we had been separated so early on in captivity had been held less than a mile away all the time we were on the rubber estate.

Terence, Sharon's young husband, walked the short distance between our camps to be reunited with his wife, only to find he was too late. I will never forget the look of utter desolation on his haggard, prematurely aged face when I broke the news to him. I couldn't even show him a grave, as Sharon was buried on Banka with my mother and many others.

This lack of an identifiable place to mark our dead was one of the hardest crosses to bear for all of us who lost loved ones.

But it was Veronica who had suffered the cruellest fate and had done so much to help keep us alive. I admired and respected her courage and was grateful for the way she put herself on the line, risking everything to help others – and ultimately sacrificing her own life.

My memory of Veronica will always be coloured by the experience of that camp. She will always be a woman of courage, of resilience and grit, unsentimental, defiant. Until the day I die myself, I will never forget watching her suffer – the protracted agony and the sudden release with Shoei's bullet.

That doesn't stop Veronica also being the woman I had known before the war. Vain, shallow, bored and bitchy. A woman who toyed with men before casting them off like worn underwear. She had played a long game of cat and mouse with men, relishing the hunt but with no desire for the feast that should normally follow the kill. And I'd hated her for what she did to Ralph.

But if I learnt one thing in those camps, it was that love sustains while hate corrodes and destroys. I can no longer hate Veronica. I feel privileged to have known her – and wish others who knew her only in peacetime had had my chance to meet that other selfless, driven woman.

PART II

LIBERTY

11

ALONE

L *ate November 1945*
I am bereft. Back in Singapore, waiting to
return to George Town, and I have never felt lone-
lier in my life. I am free from my long years of captivity, yet
there is no joy. I have lost my mother, and the death of my
father, in the labour camp where he was sent after a spell in
Changi, has been confirmed. He died in late 1944. Just three
days before Mum died.

I had suspected Dad wouldn't make it. He wasn't a strong
man, and his desk job had ill-fitted him for hard labour on
starvation rations. So, the news of his death is not what has
set me back so badly, as I had a long time to prepare for it.

What has knocked me flat and sent me into the pits of
despair is what ought to be good news.

Penny's father is alive.

I have come to love Penny as my own child and had
promised her that she would live with me and I would care
for her after the war was over. I think she loves me too. Over
those last terrible days, the worst of our entire captivity, we

sustained each other. And now she has gone, leaving a void in my life I doubt can ever be filled.

What makes me so distressed is that I don't believe Bertie Cameron really wants his daughter. He had assumed that she died along with her mother when the ship went down. He seems nonplussed by the news that she survived – although pleased to see his daughter.

Not for Bertie the suffering and privation of years in imprisonment. He spent the war re-establishing his business interests in shipping – from the comfort and safety of Australia.

He hugs Penny and smiles at her indulgently. 'Well, you clever thing, you. Fancy managing to escape from a burning ship, only to get caught by the damn Nips. Must have been absolutely frightful for you, darling.'

Yet he doesn't seem that anxious to hear more about Penny's ordeal, nor to learn any details concerning the death of her mother.

'So, poor old Weena got washed away? What a rum business.' He gives a shake of his head, brushing away the thought of his wife, blistered and blackened by sunburn, weakened by lack of food and water, being swept out to sea, while his young daughter watched, helpless. 'All over now, eh, chicken?' He pats her head awkwardly.

'What happened to you, Bertie? How did you manage to escape?' I try to keep my voice calm, level, when all I really want to do is smash my fist into his face. But he is my dear Penny's father, and is her future, so I must be circumspect.

'Luck of the devil, I suppose. Some old fishing boat came by and scooped a few of us up. We managed to get to Padang before the Japs arrived and I got on a ship to Fremantle from there. Not the pleasantest of journeys as it was rather over-crowded, but I suppose we couldn't be too picky when there was a war on.' He looks at his daughter. 'Isn't that right, darling? Eh?'

Penny stares at her feet. She is wearing a pair of sandals provided by the Red Cross. She says nothing.

I look at Bertie in his pressed linen trousers, his hair glistening with oil and his neat little moustache like a caterpillar on his top lip. I struggle not to feel contempt for him, trying to convince myself that being with her father is the best thing for Penny.

'Will you be moving back to George Town?' I ask, hoping desperately the answer is yes and that at least I will have Penny on the other side of the garden hedge again.

Bertie gives a little snorting sound. 'No, no. My future is in Australia.' He corrects himself. 'I mean *our* future. Penny will love it there.'

Penny's face is impassive. She has said nothing for several minutes.

'And to tell you the truth, Mary, I'm planning on getting married again. I've met someone out there and I'm not the kind of chap who'd get very far without a wife to keep me on my toes.' He gives a little chuckle.

Rowena never managed to keep him on his toes, nor to keep him away from the primrose path. I hope for Penny's sake that his prospective bride will have better luck keeping him from straying.

'Anyone I know?'

'No, no. She's not from the Straits. Born and bred Aussie gal.' He winks at me and I'm glad Penny doesn't see. 'She was my secretary.' He guffaws. 'Nothing like a pretty young woman to put the spring back in a chap's step.' He looks at Penny, doubtfully. 'I'm sure Betsy will be thrilled as soon as she hears this brave little thing is coming home with me.'

He turns to me and lowers his voice. 'Between you and

me, Penny's going to have a little brother or sister in the new year.' He winks at me again and I have a strong urge to slap him. 'Betsy and I rather jumped the gun, but I'm seeing her right.'

'What about your business in Penang?'

'It will be absorbed into the new Australian company. I'm still in the shipping game. Penang will be just another hub for Camerons. Our headquarters are most definitely staying in Fremantle. I may have the odd business trip back to the old island. But our life's going to be in Australia.' His tone of voice is different when he talks about business.

He looks at last directly at Penny. 'Are you excited, chicken? You should be. Wait till you see those beaches. And we'll soon get your tennis back up to scratch.'

Penny sucks her bottom lip. 'Yes, Daddy,' is all she manages.

'Time we got a move on.' Bertie jumps to his feet. I need to sort out your passage. Wasn't expecting to need another cabin. Wonderful surprise.' He turns to me and shakes my hand. 'Good show, Mary, old girl. Thanks for taking care of the lass.' He looks at his watch. 'Right-o. Tally ho!'

I clasp Penny against me, bend my head and kiss the top of hers. 'Maybe your father will manage to bring you to Penang some time on one of his business trips. You will always find a welcome with me.'

I want to ask her to tell Bertie to get lost if she'd rather live with me, but I have no right to come between a motherless child and her father.

Penny gives my bony hand a squeeze with her smaller one. 'I'll never forget you, Miss Helston. And I promise to write.' She turns to follow in her father's wake, and I am utterly alone for the first time in my life.

12

A CHANCE ENCOUNTER

J*une 1946*
    It's months since the end of the war and my return to Penang, and I still haven't returned to teaching. I'm beginning to wonder if I ever will. It's not that I don't want to, but every time I make up my mind to do so, I back out at the last minute.

Education matters enormously to me. It always has. I had managed to teach in the prison camp, despite its constraints. I enjoyed it and genuinely believe it made a difference to the children. And education is vital to the future of the country and I want to be a part of that future. Malaya's future.

I've tried to work out why I keep pulling back and postponing. The conclusion I've reached is that I have lost faith in humanity. All I want to do is scream and shout that there's no point in anything anymore when the world can allow such terrible things to happen – and, in the most part, let the guilty go unpunished.

Those Japanese prison officers who brutalised all of us will be back with their families, going about their daily lives and acting as though those years had never existed. Some of them may even have been teachers and I am pretty sure that they won't be sharing the shame of what they did with the children they are teaching, or with the mothers and fathers who have placed their children in their care. They won't even be trying to find a way to ensure it never happens again. No. They will have told themselves they were following 'superior orders' – ultimately from the emperor himself and, as such, their individual culpability has been washed away.

Obedience and duty is a central tenet of Japanese culture – even though I struggle hard not to let myself believe that cruelty is too. Those men will have wiped the war years from their consciousness, like a bad dream forgotten in the light of day. Perhaps not all of them. Some of them may have developed a conscience and tried to seek atonement, but my guess is that most of them will simply want to forget.

The Allied victors appear to feel the same. There have been only token efforts to bring men to justice – and the Emperor Hirohito and others have escaped all punishment.

How can I try to ensure that children in my care will neither be victims nor future perpetrators of crimes like that? In short, I can't. I am stuck. Frozen in time, unable to move forward and unwilling to look back. I don't want to remember, but I can't forget.

I'm probably feeling particularly glum as I now know what happened to the chosen skeleton staff at the British Military Hospital after the Japanese arrived. A doctor emerged from the hospital to greet them, carrying a white flag, and they gunned him down. A killing spree of patients and medical staff followed as the Japs rampaged through the wards, shooting and bayoneting anyone in their path. That included a patient on the operating theatre.

I think of those nurses I knew, not well, but as colleagues. Their dedication and self-sacrifice were never in question. How could God have allowed people like them to suffer in that way? Veronica Leighton too. There appears to be an inverse correspondence between an individual's readiness to help others and the cruel punishment they endure as a consequence. As long as I live, I will never understand this.

So, I remain here in my former family home, all too aware of the absence of Mum and Dad. I sit for hours in the gloom, with the shutters closed, mulling over what is past but can't be changed. I couldn't bear to move away from the bungalow, even though I am all too aware that remaining here makes my loss constantly apparent. I'd been saving up before the war and now I'm living on my savings and what was in my parents' account, so I dismissed the servants, giving them enough money to provide for their overdue retirement. It would feel wrong to have servants doing the things that I had to do for myself in the camps. And to be able to do these things of my own free will is a pleasure I hope I will never tire of.

I am missing Penny desperately. It doesn't get easier, as I had pinned all my hopes on us being together after the war. It's hard to believe that I could feel any more strongly about a child of my own. She has kept her promise to write to me, but the time that elapses between her letters is already growing longer. I am relieved and happy that she is building a new life for herself in Australia. Reading between the lines, she has little in common with Betsy, her stepmother, but Penny is overjoyed to have a new baby sister to fuss over. And while I am sure the new Mrs Cameron must have been less than thrilled to welcome a thirteen-year-old into her newly formed family, at least she has not been overtly hostile to Penny. My surrogate daughter has a growing circle of friends and plans to become a teacher when she's older. I am happy for her. But that doesn't diminish my sadness and loss. She has left a void I doubt will ever be filled.

Other people have gradually given up on me. I had never had much time for most of the expatriate women in George Town, apart from Evie. Those older ladies from Penang who were in the camp, Mum's pals, Marjorie, Beryl and Daphne, all died there. While I feel enormous kinship and love for those who survived – Laura and Cynthia among others, I have no wish to spend time with them now that we are no longer living in co-dependency. I would feel I were fetishising that period, trapped in friendships based solely on our shared incarceration. I have to make myself look to the future. And that future increasingly seems to me to be one in which the Malayan people have control over their own country.

The war has altered everything. There is a lack of trust between those left behind on Penang and those of us ordered to flee. In other words, between the locals we British abandoned, and us, their former masters. Even in the schools. My school always prided itself on taking in Malay and Chinese children, as well as those Europeans who, like Penny and her best friend, Evie's daughter, Jasmine, were not sent away to boarding school. Now the school is entirely for local children. The staff will still welcome me back, but I would no longer feel comfortable there. And even though I've suffered so much myself – perhaps more than they did – I can't help feeling guilty that they were abandoned when the Europeans were evacuated.

Some of those 'left-behind' local teachers had a terrible

war too, remaining in George Town. I know of two of them who were forcibly used as comfort women by the Japanese, even though it is never spoken of. And there was the male Malayan teacher who used to teach physical education and was beheaded as a spy after being tortured soon after the island was invaded.

We have all in our different ways witnessed the horrors of war. That is why my future will always be here in Malaya – but it will be a future of increasing self-imposed isolation. I am neither native nor European. I am dispossessed, searching for something I will never find. So here I am, rattling around an empty house, alone with my memories, my disillusionment and my despair.

I have to eat of course. My appetite might have been suppressed by the years of short rations and an almost exclusively rice diet, but I do recognise the need to buy food.

And that's how I happen to run into Reggie Hyde-Underwood outside the Cold Storage shop, where everyone in George Town buys imported food and meat.

I haven't seen Reggie since Singapore, when he'd arrived with my father, after driving him and others down from Penang – that day when I'd told him the news was confirmed that Frank was dead.

I am carrying shopping and almost knock into him in the street as I emerge from the store. I don't realise it is Reggie at first, so I mumble apologies and begin to walk away.

He calls my name. His voice is so like his brother's that for an instant I almost believe it *is* Frank. My disappointment must be evident in my face.

'I didn't know you were back in Penang,' he says. 'To be honest, I presumed you must be in England or Australia... or that maybe you hadn't made it.'

'I was in a camp.'

'Me too.'

He looks at me intently, searchingly. 'Was it bloody for you?'

I nod. 'You?'

He nods too. Then we are silent. Three and a half years of abject misery, starvation and degradation summed up in a simple word and a nod. The silence of those who know. Who have seen more than they ever want to talk about. We both start to speak at once.

I concede to him.

'Look, I'm in town for some business.' He seems nervous. 'Don't suppose you'd care to join me for a bite of supper at the E&O?'

I'm about to make an excuse. I rarely leave the house and the prospect of sitting down for a meal in a hotel doesn't appeal.

But anticipating my objections, Reggie speaks again. 'It's not like the old days. The place is looking a bit scruffy. The Japanese officers used it as their private club. The new management have only just got hold of some glasses and tableware. There was none left after all the bombing we did before the blighters surrendered. But the place is still mostly intact.' His eyes send out a silent appeal. 'It gets very lonely dining on my own, so I'd be terribly grateful if you could see your way to joining me.'

Reminding myself that he is Frank's brother, I reluctantly agree.

We don't linger talking. I am worried enough about whether I'll manage to sustain an evening's conversation with him, and I don't want to exhaust the potential topics by using them now.

On the way home, I make a diversion to buy something

to wear. Miraculously, our bungalow in George Town came through the war unscathed, our faithful servants having remained to protect the place against looters – and it had not been requisitioned by the Japanese. My clothes were all waiting in the wardrobe but, months after my liberation, they still hang off me like a child dressing up in her mother's old frocks. Even if they fitted, it would feel wrong to wear them again. They represent the old me, the one who still had hope and purpose and had known happiness and love.

In the shop, I make a decision. I will no longer wear European dress. No more cotton frocks. Malaya will always be my home so I will dress like a Malayan, not like the over-privileged white woman I had been before the war. I choose instead a simple cheongsam and a *baju kurong* – a shirt worn over a sarong.

Back home, as evening comes, I put on the silk cheongsam. It is pale jade. Very plain and unadorned. Neat enough to be respectful of my dinner companion, but not over-dressy or in any way fashionable. I stand in my bedroom and look at my reflection. I like the anonymity the garment gives me, indistinguishable from the Chinese and Malay women and quite unlike anything the *mems* would wear.

Reggie picks me up in his motorcar. It obviously isn't the one he'd had before the war. He tells me he had to dispose of that one before the invading enemy could seize it, like the car Veronica and I had seen being pushed off the dockside in Singapore. Reggie destroyed his by dowsing it in petrol and setting it on fire at the side of the Bukit Timah Road.

I'm glad he makes no comment about my dress. Reggie strikes me as not the kind of man who notices that sort of thing. He is not at all flirtatious or full of insincere charm, like so many white men. Not that anyone would give me a second glance with my straggly thin hair, rough hands and too-thin body. He probably barely notices me, and I am happy about that. On the way to the Eastern & Oriental we don't speak. It's only a ten-minute journey and I stare out of the window, grateful that he isn't trying to fill the silence.

Once we are seated at our table, Reggie with a cold beer, while I sip a fruit juice, we study the menu, both trying to prolong the period before an effort at conversation will be inevitable. That doesn't take long. It is not like the days before the war came to Penang, when the E&O served up an extensive menu of fine foods and the patrons sipped *Veuve Cliquot*, shipped in from France. Tonight, there are just one or two basic choices.

Eventually I ask him when he'd got back to Penang.

'Soon after we were liberated. I went back to England first. My wife, Susan, and our son, Stanford, had returned there from Australia after V.E. Day.' He lowers his eyes and scratches with a fingernail at the cheap cotton tablecloth that has replaced the pre-war fine linen. 'My plan had been for some R&R over there for a few months, then the three of us would head back here together. But as soon as I got to England, Susan told me she wasn't coming back to Penang.'

I listen but say nothing, waiting for him to tell me as much or as little as he wants.

'It's not even that anything bad happened to her here. She and the boy left with Evie Barrington and her two kids immediately after they got to Singapore.'

'I know. I was with them as far as Singapore.'

'Of course, you were. Sorry, I forgot that.' He smiles an apology.

'Why didn't she want to come back?'

'Susan always disliked Malaya. She's very much a home bird.' He gives a dry chuckle. 'Even Scotland's pushing it a bit for her – too many midges. She hates the climate here, the lack of seasons, the insects, everything really.'

The waiter arrives and serves us with the starters, and we begin to eat.

After a few minutes, Reggie looks up. 'When Evie's Doug died, it made matters worse. The idea that you could break your leg from a fall and die because the wound got infected in the jungle horrified her. She thought this place was savage. The Japs dropping bombs on us and forcing us to flee like thieves in the night was the last straw. She didn't like the idea of Stanford growing up here.'

'I'm sorry. Do you think she'll eventually change her mind?'

He shakes his head. 'I doubt it. She wanted me to move back there. But how could I possibly give up this life? What would I do in England? All I know about is growing rubber. I think Susan would have liked me to get a job in an office and live in a little suburban house somewhere.' He meets my eyes. 'Honestly, Mary, could you see a man like me doing that?'

I couldn't, but instead of saying so, I say, 'But didn't you both say, "for better or worse"?' As soon as I blurt the words out, I regret them. 'I'm sorry. That was uncalled for.'

'No, you're right. We did. And I certainly meant it.' He gives a long sigh and leans back in his chair. 'But war changes everything doesn't it? We'd grown up together and thought we knew each other so well but we didn't. At least it seems that way now.'

'But you have a child. Doesn't that make a difference?'

'I don't even know him, Mary. He was little more than a baby when we were separated.' He closes his eyes for a moment. 'When I was back in England, I tried, but it was hard. Being just out of the camp, I looked half-dead and the poor kid was scared of me. He didn't know me, and he didn't like the idea of this jumpy, skeletal stranger being his dad.' Reggie shakes his head again. 'Susan and I talked about Stanford coming here during the school summer break, but I could tell she wasn't keen on the idea. He wants to go to boarding school, so she'd like to have him at home with her in the holidays.' His eyes reflect his sadness. 'You probably think I'm a bad father.'

'No. I don't. Absolutely I don't. They say a child needs his father but there are countless children in the world who have lost a parent, often both of them. Once he grows up, he'll make his own decisions and before you know it, he'll be leaving home anyway and if you've given up everything, what will you have left?'

These words are more numerous than I have said to anyone since leaving the camp. It feels odd actually having a conversation. But it is odd in a good way.

We finish our starters and the waiter returns with the main course. I've only ordered a small salad with cold chicken, but this is the first meal I have actually been able to eat without pushing half of it aside.

'Maybe it's just me,' I say at last. 'But I don't like being with people who don't know what it was like for us.'

He looks up, surprised. 'Not only you. I think that was the root of the problem with Susan.' He picks up his fork then puts it down again. 'Everything she's concerned about seems to be petty and trivial.' He hesitates before blurting, 'And she didn't like the nightmares.'

'You have them too?'

He nods. 'I live it again every night. I doubt I'll ever be free of it. They liberated us physically but I'm still there mentally. Is it like that for you?'

Relief washes over me. This is the first time I have been

with someone who understands, since leaving the camp. 'It's exactly like that.'

'Apparently I wake in the night screaming. Susan kept telling me to pull myself together and get a grip, as it was scaring Stanford. Back here it's not so bad.' He frowns. Something has just occurred to him. 'Perhaps it's because *here* feels like *there*. The sounds from the jungle, the birds, the cicadas. I go to sleep and my mind and body think I'm still in the camp. In England there was none of that, so I kept going back there in my dreams.' He shakes his head. 'Does that sound crazy?'

It doesn't sound at all crazy and I tell him that.

We eat for a while in silence, but there is nothing awkward about it. I don't know Reggie well. I'd barely known him at all before I met his brother, and after that, Frank and I hadn't spent much time with him and Susan – just the odd occasion when they invited us up to Bella Vista or we met for dinner at Evie and Doug's place. We were all gathered at Evie's the night we got the phone call to say that the reason Doug was late was that he had fallen down a mineshaft and was seriously injured. Just a few days later he was dead and Evie a widow. After that, I'd spent time with her – and, whenever he could get away from the airfield, with Frank.

I like Reggie. He is very different from Frank in appearance, but they share many qualities. He seems kind, thoughtful, interested and courteous. There is a gentleness about him even though he is like a large bear. Although these days he appears a rather underfed bear – all the rather too-generous fleshiness of the old Reggie is gone, as a result of his incarceration with its physical drudgery and malnutrition. He's also lost the florid colour of his countenance. He has deep wrinkles where there was once a rotund, slightly puffy face. Anyone looking at him would recognise that he has suffered whereas in the past they would have thought he was rather too fond of his food and his *stengahs* – the ubiquitous whisky and sodas that all the ex-pat men seemed to drink.

'Are you able to talk about what happened to you?' he asks. 'Or is it too painful?'

'I've never talked to anyone and I doubt I ever will.'

He nods, his expression solemn. 'Me too.'

'They told us when they freed us from the camp that talking might help, but I can't bear the thought of sharing what I went through with anyone else.'

'I had the opposite problem. A wife whose favourite expression had become "Oh, do buck up!"'

We lapse into silence again and I look around the dining room for the first time. The once-elegant and impressive room needs repainting – re-plastering too as there are cracks in the walls and holes where the plaster is missing. The chandelier above us has only one or two functioning light-bulbs and the signature giant floral arrangements, that once stood on a marble table in the middle of the room, are gone. Some efforts have been made to brighten the place up and reclaim its reputation as the pre-eminent hotel in George Town: each table has a small posy of flowers, but the glory days of the Eastern & Oriental are long gone – perhaps forever.

There are only about a dozen other diners, scattered about the vast room. I don't recognise anyone and several of them are locals. In the heyday of the place, it had been mainly whites and one or two wealthy Chinese merchants.

Seeing me looking around, Reggie asks, 'Do you ever go to the Penang Club these days?'

'No. I never liked it and now... well, I don't actually go anywhere. Tonight's a first for me.'

Reggie smiles. 'Then I'm honoured, Mary.'

As he speaks, the band strikes up. Though depleted in numbers, they are playing the same old dance tunes from before the war.

'I didn't expect that,' he says. Impulsively, he adds, 'I say, would you like to dance?'

I am taken aback, but before I can say anything he is on his feet, pulling me onto mine. I resist the instinct to refuse and let him steer me onto the wooden dance floor, pock-marked from bomb damage or gunfire.

'I'm not a great dancer,' I say, as he begins to lead me in a waltz. 'I'm relying on you to cover up my mistakes.'

But dancing with Reggie is surprisingly relaxing and undemanding. None of the other diners have joined us, nor do they appear to show any interest in our efforts. It is strange to be dancing in a man's arms, surreal almost, after what we have both been through, yet it is oddly comforting.

The last time I had danced had been here in this very room, with Frank, the night we got engaged. It was the last time I saw him before he was killed.

The spell is broken and I drop Reggie's hold, stepping away. 'I'm sorry. I can't do this. I think I'd like to go home.'

Reggie's mouth stretches into a regretful smile. 'It's I who should be apologising. It was stupid of me. Tactless. Forgive me, Mary.'

Back at the table, he calls for the bill and we leave the restaurant. In the dark interior of his car, I feel I owe him an explanation.

'It's because of Frank. We danced together at the E&O the last time I saw him. The night he asked me to marry him.'

We are driving along the waterfront and he pulls over beside a stretch of beach and switches off the engine. 'I should have realised. That was stupid of me. Thoughtless.'

'No, it wasn't. How could you possibly have known?'

'I should have guessed that the last time you danced it would have been with him.' His head bends over the steering wheel and I sense he might be trying to hide his emotions. 'I miss him every day, Mary. He was my only brother. We had no sisters. And we got on so well, even though we were completely different. I can't even imagine what courage it must have taken to fly in those planes. He would have hated running a rubber estate with a passion. He was my little brother. Used to follow me about when he was small. I can't help thinking it's my fault he died. I was the one who encouraged him to take the posting out here rather than one in England. I thought it would be safe here. I thought it would be an adventure. I never dreamt what would happen to us all.'

'Stop!' I say. 'Never ever say such a thing again. Frank would probably have died in the summer of 1940 – I read in the paper the other day that the average life expectancy of a Spitfire pilot was four weeks. By coming to Penang he lived another eighteen months and if he hadn't come out here I'd never have met him. And of all the bloody awful, terrible things that have happened in my life, meeting Frank was not one of them.' I can hear the anger in my voice. 'I loved him and he loved me and he was and will always be the only love of my life, so don't you dare say you wish you'd never persuaded him to come here.' Tears come and they are a relief. Feeling Reggie's arms around me is a relief too.

He holds me against him, twisted around in the front seat of his car as my tears soak into his shirt. He strokes my back as I sob. When the big jerky sobs stop, I accept his starched linen handkerchief and dry my eyes.

Sniffing back the tears I say, 'That's the first time I've managed to cry properly since I left the camp. I couldn't even cry when I heard that my dad hadn't made it. So, thank you, Reggie. I feel much better already. You're the only one who understands about Frank. And I don't need to explain to you why I can't talk about what happened with the Japs, as you can't either.'

He gives me another of those tight, grim smiles – his kind face lit by the full moon reflected on the water. He flicks the starter, lets out the clutch and we set off towards my bungalow.

When we pull up outside, on a sudden impulse I ask whether he is staying in town or returning to Bella Vista, the rubber estate he manages for Evie, at the top of the island. When he says he is driving back, I find myself telling him he can stay the night and sleep in what had been my parents' room.

'You don't want to drive all the way up there in the dark. The road is probably pot-holed.'

He hesitates for a moment then says, 'If you don't mind? It's not too much trouble?'

'It will be nice to know that someone else is here in the house.'

That decides him, and he follows me up the pathway.

13

NIGHTMARE

Inside the house, I make a pot of tea and we sit at the kitchen table to drink it. Nervous and awkward, I'm starting to think I shouldn't have asked Reggie to stay the night. He might misinterpret my motives, or someone might see him leaving tomorrow morning and jump to conclusions.

As if reading my mind, he coughs. 'Maybe I should go? I shouldn't have imposed on you, Mary. I'd intended to stay at the E&O but they only have a few rooms open so far and those were all taken. I'll drive back to Bella Vista tonight. It's not that late and I know the road well.'

I can tell he doesn't really want to go. His face shows his tiredness.

'Don't be daft, Reggie. I told you, I'm glad of the company. The bed in my parents' room is made up anyway, so it's no trouble at all – you might as well make use of it. And how could I live with myself if you were found in your car at the bottom of a gully tomorrow?'

He leans back in his chair and drinks his tea.

For some reason, I don't want him to go. His presence is

reassuring. Reggie is a thoroughly nice man. Decent. I like to think Frank would approve if he could see me here, sharing a companionable cup of tea with his brother. And he would also be pleased that I had managed to get out of the house tonight and do something normal for once.

I look up and see Reggie is studying my face.

'You look thoughtful,' he says.

'I was thinking about Frank. You're like him in many ways.'

Reggie gives me a rueful smile. 'Certainly not in appearance. Old Frank got the lion's share of the good looks in our family.'

I wish I hadn't brought the subject up, as it would be hard to disagree with him. No one would describe Reggie as handsome, whereas Frank fitted the template of the dashing RAF pilot, with film star good looks. But Reggie has kind eyes. And a nice smile.

'I can't imagine why you'd think that.' My voice sounds awkward and he must realise I'm being disingenuous.

'I'm not fishing for compliments, Mary.' He gives me a grin. 'I never envied my brother's good looks. Since Susan was my childhood sweetheart the lack never bothered me – I didn't go chasing after the girls.'

I laugh. 'And Frank did?'

'Frank didn't have to – they all chased after him. Not that he was interested. Until he met you, I'd begun to think he'd never want to settle down.'

Noticing he's finished his tea, I pour us both another cup.

'What I meant when I said you were like Frank, is you're a good listener. That's unusual in men. Mostly they either glaze over, as though what you're talking about isn't important enough to merit their full attention, or they talk over the top of you, constantly cutting in as if what they have to say is far more important.'

'Then most men are fools.' He smiles.

Ignoring what I take to be a compliment, I say, 'I've always found that odd, the way so many men – and to be fair, some women too – love the sound of their own voice, even though, by definition, since they're telling it, they already know the story. Frank wasn't like that at all. He was genuinely curious. He loved people. I get the feeling you do too.'

He looks embarrassed and I wish I hadn't said all that. It would be dreadful if he mistook what I was saying as flirtation.

To change the subject, I ask him about the rubber estate. He tells me he's working hard to restore its fortunes.

'The coolies fled when we were evacuated, and the Japanese didn't bother with Bella Vista. I've promised Evie I'll work like a Trojan until I've got it back to how it was before the war.'

'I doubt Evie needs the money.' I can hear the bitterness in my own voice. The war, and her avoidance of it in Australia, has made me resent her – like everyone who was fortunate enough to escape – even though I know it's not her fault that I didn't. 'She has income from the other rubber estate too, the one near Butterworth.'

'She's considering an offer for the other place. Although I think she should hold out for a better one. It can't be easy for a widow with two children.'

His generosity of spirit shames me. After all, Evie is my best friend and has shown nothing but kindness to me.

Before I can answer, Reggie adds, 'Our house at Bella Vista was unoccupied during the war. Too far out of town for the Japs. But it wasn't in bad order considering.' He grins. 'Remember when we were all leaving Penang? We were told no pets, and everyone had to shoot their dogs at the harbour as they weren't allowed to leave with us.'

I'd forgotten, but now remembered the horrible scene at the dockside.

'I had Badger, Doug's dog. Doug told Evie he wanted me to take care of the dog, once he knew he was dying.'

'Of course. Now I remember. Did you have to shoot the poor thing?'

'Thankfully no. I was in a terrible quandary – I would have felt I was letting Doug down – and I was fond of the dog. Our houseboy had driven down to the harbour with us to help with the bags. He took Badger back to Bella Vista and somehow managed to keep him alive throughout the war, despite all the shortages. I couldn't believe it when I got back and there he was, wagging his tail.'

'How lovely.'

'Yes. It's made such a difference to me having Badger. Dogs are such loyal and undemanding companions.'

I could see the loneliness in his eyes and was glad he had the dog. Bella Vista was isolated, up high at the top of the island.

'Was everything else all right when you returned?'

'Surprisingly, yes, considering we all shipped out in such a hurry. It was just as we'd left it. Apart from the dust and the dead insects. Amil, our houseboy, and the other servants who remained, had locked the house up and stayed in their own quarters. Susan's orchid garden suffered though.'

'I'd forgotten your wife grew orchids.'

'Her pride and joy. They've reverted to the state they were in when she and I moved into Bella Vista. Left to run rampant. Fighting it out with creepers and trees trying to choke them. Almost four years is a long time in this climate. The jungle takes over so quickly.'

'Will you try to restore the orchid garden?'

He raises his eyebrows. 'Can't see that happening. Vegetables are more my thing. A few of us made a little vegetable plot in the camp, cultivating plants from scraps and roots. It supplemented our diet – until the Japs realised what we were up to, told us to dig everything up and hand the lot over to them.'

'Did you try again?'

'No. That area became our burial ground instead.' His mouth tightens.

I look away. I don't want to talk about the camps, and I am afraid he might change his mind and ask me about my experiences. But he doesn't.

'A woman from the Red Cross came to see me a few months back,' I say. 'She wanted to encourage me to talk. I think it was the doctor's idea – he says I'm depressed. But I didn't want to talk to her.' I meet his eyes. 'Everyone asks about the camp. What it was like being held by the Japs. Everyone apart from you – you don't need to. And the irony is when they ask, they don't really want to know. They just want to mend us, like broken dolls, put us back together again so we can all go back to normal and pretend it never happened. But we'll never be normal again, will we, people like you and me?'

'I don't know.' He looks baleful. 'You're right about people not really wanting to know. That just about sums up Susan's attitude. She wanted what happened to be swept under the carpet so that we could get on with the rest of our lives. My dirty little secret.' He drops his head. 'Anyway, how can you tell someone who's never been there just how bad it was? It's not fair to inflict that on other people.'

He puts down his cup and it rattles in the saucer. 'I got a letter from Susan last week. She wants a divorce. Says she's met someone else.' He closes his eyes so I can't see the pain and hurt I am sure are in them. 'He's a farmer. A widower.'

'I'm sorry, Reggie.' I touch his hand lightly but don't let it linger there. 'How do you feel about that?'

'It's so final. I suppose it was inevitable, but it still came as a huge shock. I thought that maybe if it was just a separation there was always the possibility...' His voice trails away. 'But perhaps it's for the best. Susan wants to get on with her life and it will force me to get on with mine.'

He releases a long sigh that indicates his words aren't even convincing himself. 'We'd been together since we were kids, Susan and I. We'd always known one day we'd marry. And she was such a...a lovely woman.' His voice breaks. 'I loved her – I really loved her – until...until all this bloody mess of a war. But it's impossible to keep on loving someone when you grow as far apart as we have. When I try to remember how it used to be with us, it seems like a story, not something that actually happened. And maybe the signs were already there before the war.'

He stares into the middle distance. 'Susan and I are too different. I should have realised that when she was so miserable here in Penang, when I love the place so much. But I refused to acknowledge her misery, even to myself, much less to her. Both of us kept trying to pretend that it would be all right in the end. Perhaps the war did us a service. Saved us years of living a lie and growing further apart.' He turns back to look directly at me. 'I've talked enough. You're a good listener, Mary. Thank you. But I need to get to bed. I have to make an early start in the morning.'

· · ·

I AM awoken by terrible cries. At first, I think I'm having a nightmare – that I am back in the camp and Sergeant Shoei is screaming at me for not bowing low enough. I realise the cries are coming from the front bedroom. This isn't a scream of anger, but of abject terror.

Without hesitation, I jump out of bed and run in my nightgown along the landing and open the door to the other bedroom. Reggie is lying on his side in the bed, his body in a foetal position, his arms shielding his head. The screaming has changed to a low monotonous moan.

I move across to the bed. It isn't a conscious decision so much as an instinctive reaction. It is one human being responding to the cry for help of another. Easing back the sheet, I climb onto the bed behind Reggie and curl my body into his, holding him in my arms, cradling him. It is more the act of a mother towards her child. A response to his pain and loneliness – and – although I don't allow myself to admit it – to my own.

Neither of us speaks. We lie together in the dark bedroom and gradually his breathing calms. I am not even sure whether he knows I am here. He may still be asleep. I drift away into a deep and dreamless sleep myself.

When someone has been married for a long time, they must be used to the familiar presence of their spouse beside them in the bed at night. Perhaps it's quite normal for them to make love while still half asleep. I don't know. I've never been married. In fact, I've never slept in a bed with a man or made love. When Reggie turns over and draws me into his arms, I don't know what to make of it. It is too dark to see his face.

As I feel his mouth on mine and his erection pressing up against my body, I could stop him. What on earth is he thinking? This is wrong. It is not supposed to happen. And yet, I let him hold me, his strong arms wrapped around me, holding me so close that I can feel his heart beating against my own. I should get out of the bed, explain why I have come to be there in the first place, and go back to my own room. He would apologise, tell me he wasn't aware of what he was doing, perhaps that he has mistaken me for his wife in that half-life between sleep and consciousness. Neither of us would have mentioned it ever again.

But I don't do that. I not only let him make love to me, my body responds to him. I have never made love before. Ralph and I had agreed to wait until we were married. After his death, when I met Frank and we fell in love, I made up my mind that I would give myself to him at the first opportunity. What had happened to Ralph convinced me that life was too brief to do anything other than grab at any happiness along the way. That last evening together when Frank asked me to marry him, he'd booked a room at the E&O. But our plans were dashed when he got an urgent telephone call to return to his base at Butterworth immediately. I never saw him again. He was killed days later.

While I've never made love before, I am not without experience of sexual intercourse.

Here, in my parents' bed in that darkened room, my decision to let Reggie do what he wants to do might be a way to help wash away those terrible memories of that Japanese soldier. Reggie's lovemaking might be the only way to ease the horror of what happened to me that day, to show my body that this act doesn't have to be one of power and punishment.

Nor does it have to be born of lust or passion. Instead, what we are doing tonight arises from our mutual loneliness, a shared tragedy and a need for solace. It is tender, warm and soothing. We do not speak. There is no need for words.

When it is over, I lie there beside him in the dark silent bedroom. As soon as I am sure he is calm and asleep, I swing my legs over the side of the bed and patter back along the landing to my own bedroom. I lie in the now-cooled bed, and realise I am smiling. I have not felt so at peace since I returned to Penang. I drift back to sleep myself.

In the morning, I wake just after seven, and sense that Reggie has gone. The door to my parents' bedroom is open and he isn't in the bed. I move across to the window and draw the curtain back. His car has gone.

I feel the blood rushing to my cheeks as I remember the events of last night. I am embarrassed when I think about what has taken place between us, but I don't regret it. It was an instinctive need for closeness, and I feel calmer and more purposeful than I have in months – no, years. I hope Reggie will feel the same way. Not that I want to repeat what we've done. He is still a married man and I am the former fiancée of his brother. A romance between us is out of the question. In fact, a romantic liaison with anyone is out of the question for me. Two dead fiancés is two too many. I've long ago reached the conclusion that I am cursed where love and marriage are concerned. No, I am grateful for the way I felt wrapped in a warm cocoon when Reggie held me and made love to me, but we will never repeat it.

I go into the bathroom and run a bath. Finding, at the back of a cupboard, a bottle of perfumed bath oil from before the war, I pour some into the water and breathe in the scent of jasmine. It is the first time I've indulged myself this way. All those years of being unwashed and filthy have made the idea of adding potions and lying in a warm bath feel too sybaritic. It would have been an insult to the memory of all the women I had lost in the camps including my mother.

But as I lie here with the sweet-scented water around me, I think of Veronica. She would have had no time for such self-flagellation. I can imagine her saying, 'Don't be silly, darling, you deserve it. Why not treat yourself?' I smile, as I reflect she would probably also have sniffed at my choice of bath oil and told me where I could find a much more luxurious and expensive one.

Downstairs, I make tea and eat a piece of toast. All too often I skip breakfast – three meals a day seems excessive after the years of starvation. But today I have an appetite. After washing up the plates, I take a book at random off the shelf in the parlour and instead of staying in there and shutting myself away, as usual, in the cool gloom, I go outside and sit in the garden.

I open the book. It's a poetry collection. *Sonnets from the Portuguese* by Elizabeth Barrett Browning. I have never been a great lover of poetry but feel too lethargic to get up and venture back inside for something else. As I skim through the pages this verse catches my eye.

> *The face of all the world is changed, I think,*
> *Since first I heard the footsteps of thy soul*
> *Move still, oh, still, beside me, as they stole*
> *Betwixt me and the dreadful outer brink*
> *Of obvious death, where I, who thought to sink,*
> *Was caught up into love, and taught the whole*
> *Of life in a new rhythm.*

I LET the book fall shut into my lap, uncomfortable with the words I have read, wishing I had never seen them.

I don't hear the car pull up outside and only gradually become aware of knocking at the front door. I go inside and open it and Reggie is standing there.

Trying to hide my shock and discomfort I say, 'Come in. I was in the garden.'

He follows me through the house and out onto the patchy neglected lawn. I offer him a cold drink, but he declines.

'I had to speak to you,' he says. 'All the way back to Bella Vista this morning I was thinking I shouldn't have left like that. Without saying goodbye. Without so much as a word. When I got home, I was going to write or telephone you, but I decided I need to speak to you face-to-face.'

His cheeks are red with embarrassment and I can feel my own turning the same colour.

I start to reply but he interrupts me.

'Did you come to my bed last night?'

I bite my lip but nod to acknowledge that I had.

'Was it out of pity? Did you think it would be a consolation prize after I told you about Susan?' His voice is jumpy, nervous. 'Please tell me. Did you seduce me because you felt sorry for me?'

I am aghast. 'I didn't seduce you. Your screaming woke me up. I was concerned about you. You were having a nightmare, so I got into the bed and held you until you calmed. That was all.'

He lets out a sigh. 'Nothing happened? We didn't...?'

The lie is out of me before I can stop it. It is much easier. Much kinder, much less complicated than telling him the truth. 'No, we didn't. Nothing happened. After a while you fell asleep. I went back to bed and when I woke up you'd gone.'

Reggie grins, his relief palpable.

I feel quite insulted – but I am hardly an attractive prospect with my thinning hair, rough hands and skinny body with its little pot belly.

Before I can say anything else, he reaches for my hands and holds them in his. 'Only I'd hate to get off on the wrong foot with you, Mary. I've been worried sick all morning that I might have... you know... taken advantage of you. I'd like to see you again. I'm not a free man until my divorce is finalised, but I hope we might spend more time with each other in the meantime and then who knows...' His voice trails away.

I stare at him, taken aback. I hadn't expected that at all.

'Only I think we got on rather well last night,' he says. 'We have a lot in common with what we've both been through. I could never replace Frank for you, but maybe, in time, we might make a go of things. I know I can only be second best. I don't expect more.'

I am still tongue-tied.

'I'm no great shakes in the good looks department, but I'm a hard worker and a good provider. We're both lonely and I'd like to take care of you.' He looks at me intently. 'You haven't said anything. I've embarrassed you, haven't I? I've rushed things and frightened you. I don't want to put you under any pressure. Just give me a chance, Mary. Let's see how it goes. One day at a time.'

I swallow. I hate to burst his bubble, but I have to do it. 'I'm sorry, Reggie. I can't. It's not you. It's me. There's a curse over me. I'm the woman who's had two fiancés and both died on me. I can't go through all that again. I'll never marry. I don't want to have that kind of relationship anymore. Too much pain. Too much heartbreak. I *want* to be alone. It suits me.' My voice sounds cold, sharp, even to me.

His face falls, and he drops my hands. 'I see,' he says. 'I'm sorry. I thought...Goodbye.' He walks back to the house, his shoulders hunched. At the French windows, he turns back to face me, 'Please forget this ever happened. I won't bother you again. I'm sorry, Mary.'

After he's gone, I sit in the chair, gazing into space. What I'd said was the truth, so why do I have this hollowed out, empty feeling? Why do I have the desire to weep?

14

THE VISITOR

December 1946

After my encounter with Reggie, I started to write my memoir of what happened to me in Singapore and after. I needed a project to fill the long empty days. And I needed something to take my mind off what happened with Reggie Hyde-Underwood.

Getting the words onto paper was a strange experience. I dreaded doing it, but the process proved to be cathartic. Reliving what had happened to me in those long terrible years of the war, helped me to remove myself from it. Writing it down made those experiences seem to have happened to someone else, someone outside of me, like watching a film show. Remembering, recording, then letting go, made me feel at once calmer and at peace.

I STILL HAVEN'T RETURNED to teaching at the school. I have a sense that the place they are holding for me probably doesn't exist; that they are paying lip service to my stated intention to return to work and we all know it will never happen. Besides, the school seems to be functioning fine without me. There are significantly fewer European pupils than before the war – many mothers, like Susan and Evie, have returned with their children to Britain. It will doubtless take a new generation of white children to be born out here before the numbers return to their pre-war levels – if indeed they ever do.

The writing of my war memoir has filled my days until now. If I am not going to teach again, I will need to find some other form of employment. I am still living on my meagre savings and Mum and Dad's more substantial, but still modest ones. You have to hand it to the British, they may have been a disaster at hanging onto Singapore but they are highly skilled at running and preserving banking systems. Yet even though my funds are there and accessible, they will not last for long. I refuse to let myself think about that yet. I shall be like Mr Micawber and assume that 'something will turn up'.

THIS MORNING I wake to sunshine cutting through a gap between the faded bedroom curtains, washing a pale light across the bedroom floor. From outside I can hear birdsong. There is something so normal and ordinary about it. This is the first time I have woken and not travelled back in time to the camps. The heavy weight of sadness that has dragged me down since I returned to Penang has at last lifted – at least temporarily. I find I am smiling and filled with hope. It's not a specific feeling, but a general sense of wellbeing – of being in the right place and feeling secure. After washing, I go downstairs, eat some toast and drink my way through a pot of strong tea. Such simple pleasures are still such a luxury to me after the years of drinking brown rice coffee and eating rice porridge.

But I won't let myself think about all that today. I no longer need to. My memoir is written, and safely stowed away at the bottom of an old leather suitcase on top of the wardrobe. I have written it out of my life and have broken free of the burden my time in the camps placed upon me.

Yesterday, I wrote to the school confirming that I will not be returning to teach there. I thought I'd feel bereft, but another weight has lifted from my shoulders.

As I finish washing the few dishes, there's a knock on the front door. Surprised, I get up but delay going to answer it. No one comes to call on me these days. I stand behind the door, trying to make up my mind whether to open it. Hoping it's not someone from the school, wanting to change my mind, I tell myself I am being ridiculous and open the door tentatively.

Evie Barrington is standing on the path, looking up at my bedroom window. She must have imagined I was still in bed as the curtains are still closed. I am stunned at seeing her. Surprise turns to joy and I open my arms and embrace her, holding her tall frame against my gaunt misshapen body. For I am still that oddity, a wraithlike creature with a swollen rice belly and puffy ankles in a body that is otherwise a bag of bones. Evie hugs me back, as happy to see me as I am to see her.

'Look at you!' she says. 'Wearing a sarong. Quite the native.' She gives me a warm smile.

We go through into the garden, where we drink real coffee, sitting under a frangipani tree, the sweet scent wrapping around us.

'How I love being here,' Evie says, waving her hand through the air in an expansive gesture.

The garden is neglected, overgrown, the lawn a bare dry patch, the plants rampant, yet the tree flowers are even more profuse than they were before the war.

'Everything is so lush, so colourful. Everywhere smells so...so exotic. London is filthy and full of thick smog. It's impossible to breathe. I couldn't wait to be back here.'

'But what brings you back to Penang? You told me you were going to live in England. What's happened to change your mind?' My heart lifts at the prospect of having Evie back in George Town.

'Everything's changed, Mary!' She is grinning, bubbling over with joy. I don't think I have ever seen her so happy. For a moment I feel a twinge of jealousy.

'I'm not here for good. Just long enough to sort out some things with the solicitor and with Reggie.' She takes my hands in hers. 'I'm getting married, Mary!'

I gaze at her open-mouthed.

'Married? Who to?' For one terrible breath-stopping moment I think she is about to tell me it's Reggie. And I don't like the thought of that at all. Not one little bit.

She looks at me and grins. 'Arthur Leighton of course. Who else?'

My eyes widen. 'He's alive? You found him?'

'All my detective work came to nothing. It was Jasmine who found him for me. We were having tea in Lyons Corner House and she spotted him through the window. What was the chance of that happening?'

I am still trying to absorb this information. I had assumed that Arthur must be dead, and Evie was deluding herself in her conviction that he had survived the war.

'Why hadn't he contacted you?'

Evie gives me a knowing look. 'Things were very tough for Arthur in the war. He went through a horrible ordeal and afterwards he thought I wouldn't want to be with him because of all the terrible things that happened to him. He was filled with self-loathing.' She gives her head a little shake, conveying her incredulity that he could ever have thought such a thing. I, for my part, know all too well how Arthur must have felt.

'But as soon as we saw each other again, it was all right. He and I have always known we were meant to be together.'

I remember what Veronica had said to me that afternoon in the camp. About how hard it was for her to discover she loved her husband, only to realise that it was too late, and he loved someone else. Now I know that someone else was Evie.

'I loved Arthur from the moment I first set eyes on him on the quayside in Tilbury, when he and Veronica travelled out to Penang with me the first time. I just didn't want to admit it to myself. He felt the same. Those two years I was married to Douglas, and the year after he died before the war began, I was desperate not to let myself admit I loved Arthur. I had tried so hard to make my marriage work and after that to honour Doug in death. Arthur wasn't the kind of man who would walk out on his marriage – especially when Veronica was so fragile and needy.' She studies the back of her hands for a moment, then lifts her head to look at me. 'You know that, as well as having a problem with alcohol, Veronica suffered from terrible bouts of depression? Suicidal.'

I nod. 'We became close in the prison camp.' I give her a sad smile. 'Odd as that friendship may seem. Veronica was a complex woman. I'd never have come through those three-and-a-half years if it were not for her.'

'Did she ever speak of Arthur?'

I hesitate. 'She told me she realised too late how much she cared for him, but she knew he was in love with someone else. Oh Evie, I'd no idea it was you. She wouldn't tell me who it was.'

She nods. 'Poor Veronica,' she says. 'Arthur said she knew. He always claimed he owed his career to her. She worked tirelessly to play the part of the Foreign Service wife.'

I think of how Veronica had played the courtesan to Sergeant Shoei. How she had told me about her past infidelities and how she used her body to gain advantage. 'Veronica was a great fixer. An organiser. And the person most responsible for keeping my spirits up in captivity.'

I take Evie's hand. 'But she was never right for Arthur. Just as Doug was never right for you.' I smile, pleased for her. Now that my memoir is done, I can afford to be generous about her good fortune. I have put the bitterness and anger behind me.

Evie is paler. The English climate has bleached away the tropical sun from her skin. But her happiness is so evident that she looks beautiful, glowing, radiant.

She reaches again for my hand. 'We're going to live in Africa. Arthur has accepted a position with the Colonial Office, working in Kenya. He's already out there. I've stayed in England to sort things out – the children's schooling, Doug's affairs, that kind of thing. That's why I'm here in George Town.'

While I'm disappointed that she won't be moving back to Penang, I am genuinely happy for Evie. I really am. Happy for the children too and for Arthur. The more I think about it, the more I have to acknowledge they are indeed perfect for each other. I tell her that.

'Thank you, Mary.' She squeezes my hand. 'So, when are you going to tell me about the baby?' She gives me a little nudge.

I look at her, puzzled. 'What baby?'

She touches my distended stomach. 'This one, silly.'

I sigh. 'That's not a baby. It's my rice belly. It won't go away.'

She raises her eyebrows. 'I know what a rice belly is. Arthur had one, a little round pot, but it didn't take long on a normal balanced diet for it to disappear. That, my darling, is not a rice belly. You can't fool me. I'm a mother, remember?' She reaches for my hand, but I draw it away before she can grasp it.

'I don't know what you're talking about. It's impossible.'

'Have you seen a doctor?'

I shake my head, shocked at the import of her words.

'When was your last period?'

'I don't have them. They stopped when I was imprisoned. It happened to us all.'

'But since you were liberated? They must have started again?'

I feel the blood drain from my face. My hands are shaking. 'I did have one or two. But very light. Almost nothing. Then nothing at all for a long time.' I look at her. I am in shock. 'Months.'

'I'd hazard a guess you are at least six months gone. And the father?' she asks, gently.

I start to cry. She passes me an embroidered linen handkerchief and puts her arm around me. 'You can trust me, Mary. No matter what the circumstances. You are my dearest friend and I love you. I will always support you.'

'I had no idea, Evie. Are you sure?'

She smiles. 'Pretty positive, but I'm not a doctor. Would you like me to come with you to the surgery?'

I nod, still numb with shock. 'It was only one time. It just happened. We had dinner. It was late and I offered him my parents' room to stay over so he wouldn't have to drive home in the dark. In the night he was screaming. A nightmare. The camps. I went into his room to calm him. One thing led to another.' I look up at Evie, terrified, my voice barely a whisper. 'It was only once!'

'That's all it takes sometimes.' Evie stretches her mouth into a grim smile. 'Don't worry, I'm sure everything will be fine. I'm here for you, Mary...' She hesitates but, knowing what she's about to ask, I cut in to preempt the question. I want to get it over.

'It was Reggie.'

She looks at me, incredulous. 'Reggie Hyde-Underwood?' As if there was another Reggie who it could possibly be. She clamps a hand over her mouth. 'And he has no idea?' She starts to laugh. 'What are you two like? Reggie's a father, for heaven's sake. He should have been able to tell just by looking at you.'

'He hasn't seen me. Not since it happened.'

Evie expels a long sigh. 'What are we going to do with you, Mary? You have to tell him immediately. It's his child. Doesn't he deserve to know?'

I still can't believe this is happening. 'Reggie's a married man. And...' I want to say I don't love him but the slow realisation is finally dawning that maybe I do.

Instead I say, 'He doesn't even remember. He thought he'd dreamt it. What we did that night. I told him nothing happened.' A wave of misery washes over me. What must Evie think of me? Susan Hyde-Underwood is a friend of hers. They were in Australia together. Evie must see me as a marriage-breaker.

Apparently reading my mind, Evie says, 'Susan is getting married to a chap from Yorkshire. He's a widowed farmer with two small children. When I first met her and Reggie, I thought they had a perfect marriage. They seemed so attuned to each other, but gradually I began to see that it wasn't quite like that. It was a mutual awareness that arose from habit, from growing up together. Not from love.'

Evie pauses. I can tell she's weighing up how much to tell me. 'Susan hated Penang. And that bad feeling about the place intensified with the war and, since Reggie loves it so much here, the animosity she felt for Malaya gradually transferred into her feelings about him. That's why she wouldn't move back here. It wasn't just her aversion to the place, it had become an aversion to the man.'

She stops, gets up from the wooden chair where she is sitting beside me, and starts to pace up and down. 'I probably shouldn't be telling you this, but I'm going to anyway. Yes, Susan is a friend but not in the way *you* are. It's important that you understand this so that you don't sacrifice your own happiness in some cockeyed attempt to be honourable.' She stops pacing and stands in front of me. 'Susan had an affair while we were in Australia. It was with one of the doctors at the hospital where we were helping out. His wife found out and he broke it off with Susan. There was a bit of a scandal.'

'My goodness. *Susan*? I'd never have expected that.'

'No. I didn't either. I found out because there was quite a bit of gossip. I defended her when it reached me and thinking she ought to know what was being said behind her back, I told her about what I believed to be scurrilous rumours, expecting her to be as horrified as I was. But she laughed and told me it was all true. She said it had only been a fling. That she was fed up living like a nun and had picked Dr Morley simply because he was married and was happy for it to be just about the sex.'

My mouth is gaping open. This is so unlike what I had thought Susan to be – a quiet, loyal *mem*, the classic planter's wife – only a *mem* who didn't actually like the fact that her husband was a planter. The idea of her deliberately having an affair, regardless of the consequences, stuns me. While she was doing it, poor Reggie was suffering unspeakable atrocities during his internment. I suddenly hate Susan with a passion.

'I had no idea,' I say. 'I would never have expected that of Susan.'

Evie shakes her head slowly. 'Me neither. To be honest, Mary, I've not been comfortable with her since. Our boys are friends, so I've had to keep up the friendship with her, but I was jolly glad when she said she was going to be living in Yorkshire.'

We lapse into silence. 'So, what are we going to do about you and Reggie?' she says at last. 'Do you care for him?'

I feel a sob rising in my throat again and push it back down. I have to stay calm. 'I don't know, Evie. I didn't think so. After all, he was Frank's brother. It doesn't seem right.'

'Frank's gone,' she says quietly. 'And Frank loved you both and would want you both to be happy above all else.' She places a hand on my swollen abdomen. 'Besides you need to think about your child. He or she will need a father. And Susan's deprived Reggie of being anything other than a distant one to Stanford.'

I take a gulp of air. 'The next day, the morning after it happened, Reggie told me he wanted us to spend time together and hinted that he hoped it might eventually lead to something more. I told him it was out of the question. I sent him away.' A tear runs down my cheek into the corner of my mouth. 'I was horrible. Mean. Cold. I haven't seen him since. Oh, Evie, I've messed everything up.'

'Don't be silly,' she says in a stern voice. 'It's not too late. Reggie is one of the nicest men I know. And you and he will be perfect together.' She claps her hands together. 'Right, we need to get you to the doctor and find out your due date. Then you need to take yourself up to Bella Vista and tell Reggie he is going to be a father.

15

BELLA VISTA

Evie is right. The doctor says I am six months' pregnant. Now that the truth has been confirmed, I wonder how I managed to delude myself for so long that my swelling stomach was the continuing effect of rice belly. Since liberation, I'd been unable to bear eating another grain of the stuff, so what did I think was causing my stomach to keep swelling?

I suppose I haven't been able to confront the truth. And I am still not sure I can. Part of me continues to believe I've done something wrong. As the former fiancée of Reggie's brother, I can't help thinking I've committed a sin by allowing what passed between us to happen. In making love with Reggie, I have betrayed Frank.

Fear is at the bottom of all my doubts and my self-dissembling. I am afraid to grasp hold of happiness, since it has always been true that, as soon as I have had it in my hand, it has been torn away from me. Perhaps I'm not worthy of being happy and that is the reason it has eluded me. My internment has made me fearful, unwilling to trust, unsure of myself and my emotions.

The idea of becoming a mother terrifies me. Bringing a child into a world where such horrible things as happened to me could happen again. And, having witnessed those things, they might have destroyed my capacity to be a loving mother.

But most of all, I am afraid to admit that perhaps I might actually love Reggie.

He is not the kind of man I would usually be drawn to. I paid him little or no attention until his brother's courtship of me brought him directly into my orbit – and even then, our encounters consisted of little more than polite exchanges. He was just another chap from the club. Just another rubber planter. If I had thought of Reggie at all, it was that he was a bland but pleasant man, not particularly attractive, and that we probably had little in common beyond the fraternal connection. He fell into the large and unexplored category of rather dull married men.

Yet as I feel the child inside me quicken, I can't stop thinking about the night he and I spent together. I have never before felt such tenderness for another human being and experienced it being shown to me. My affinity with Reggie is not logical, nor born of strong physical attraction. It goes much deeper. As if we are viscerally connected. Beyond logic, beyond reason. Maybe in the final analysis that's why I am so scared.

EVIE OFFERS to accompany me up to Bella Vista, but I tell her this is something I have to do alone. My wonderful, kind friend tells me she will drive me up there and leave me to get on with it.

'It can't be easy driving a car with that belly between you

and the steering wheel,' she says, grinning. 'I'll drop you off and make myself scarce.'

She gives me a sly grin. 'But I hope to see you later tonight. Reggie's arranged to come into George Town to have dinner at my house to discuss the estate. You can both come.' She winks at me, pointing a finger. 'And never mind the estate business, I want to be the first person you two tell.'

I start to protest. 'He may not want me... he may–'

'Rubbish! You are about to make him the happiest man in Penang.'

I wish I shared Evie's confidence, but I am swept along by her enthusiasm. I say a silent prayer that she's right. Because, to my great surprise, now that this is out in the open, I realise that there is nothing more I want than to be with Reggie. The thought of seeing him soon fills me with a mixture of terror and longing.

Evie drives through the gates to Bella Vista and drops me just short of the *padang,* where the daily roll call of the coolies is done. I can't help being reminded of the *tenko* on that other rubber estate, the scene of Veronica's death in Sumatra.

But the atmosphere is different up here at Bella Vista. The sun lights up the ground and the heat is tempered by the altitude and the gentle breeze coming up off the straits. And the coolies – mostly Tamils from South India and Ceylon – have never been expected to bow to the *tuan,* have always been paid for their labour and are free to come and go, to live with their families and to have plenty of food in their stomachs.

As I walk across the open stretch of land, I see him – the *tuan besar* of Bella Vista, Reggie Hyde-Underwood.

He is standing outside one of the large wooden huts where they roll out the latex into sheets, ready for transporting to the godowns in George Town. Doug's old dog – and he must be very old – is beside him. After all these months, Reggie appears taller than I remember. He is still thin, rangy, none of his pre-war fleshiness has returned. My stomach does a flip – a combination of nerves and desire.

He turns, sees me, does a double take, and runs towards me, the dog shambling along behind him. He slows to a walk as he gets closer, his surprise and nervousness about my sudden unannounced appearance, evident on his face.

'Mary.' He says my name and it speaks a thousand words.

I look at him and see the uncertainty in his eyes.

Taking a long, slow breath, trying to control my shaking, I say, 'I'm having a baby. It's your baby. I mean *we* are having a baby, Reggie. Soon.'

I am struggling to find the right words, when Reggie takes away the need for any words at all by taking me into his arms and kissing me. A long, slow, beautiful kiss. I stand here, on the wide expanse of the *padang,* as he kisses me again, and keeps on kissing me. I wrap myself in his warmth and tenderness.

When at last we emerge from the kiss, he asks, 'Will you marry me, Mary?'

All I can do is grin. The widest, happiest grin I have ever made.

EPILOGUE

April 1948

Our baby is a girl. Now a year old. We called her Frances. Apart from her first name being the female version of Frank's given name, it means 'free one'. That strikes me as a singularly appropriate name for the first child of two former prisoners of war. I hope and pray that she will live in a different world from the one her parents experienced. That she will be part of a new freer future for the country that is our home.

Frances is a lively baby. Strong and healthy. Already a year old and able to stand on her chubby wobbly legs. Beautiful – with a mop of light brown hair and eyes of the most beautiful hazel green. She is a miracle. After the years of starvation and suffering I still can't believe my body was capable of conceiving and bearing a child.

Reggie is a devoted father. He is besotted with his daughter. Just as – to my constant astonishment – he is besotted with me. And I with him.

I had believed his brother to be the love of my life, but I was wrong. Frank was and will always be dear to my heart

and I will always love him. But with Reggie I have found my
true soul mate. The joy of finding such a deep and enduring
love, when I had abandoned all hope of it, is all the sweeter.
Every day I send up my thanks to God or the universe – my
faith is flexible – that we found each other. We are different
in so many ways, yet that in itself is the source of the joy we
take in each other's company.

We never speak of the war. We never need to. Both of us
instinctively knows when the other is feeling low, when the
bad memories encroach. We are there with each other, for
each other. He is the balm to my troubled soul. When I
experience the occasional day of utter despair and sadness,
Reggie senses it and knows not to ask questions, but to hold
me, to love me, to heal me. And I him.

I have begun teaching again. Not at my old school down
in George Town, but up here in the nearby *kampong*. I am
teaching the children of the coolies and the local villagers to
read and write in English – something that will stand them
in good stead for the future. I bring Frances with me to the
hut where I hold the lessons and one of the mothers cares
for her while I take the class.

I am not without anxiety for the future. The communists
and nationalists have been growing in influence in Malaya
since the war and it feels the unrest might be coming to a
head. The Japanese did all they could to foment this – with
their 'Asia for the Asians' propaganda. And to be honest, I
am not unsympathetic. This country rightly belongs to its
indigenous people. Not to us British interlopers. Not to the
big British, American, Dutch and French rubber companies.
I hope we will find a way to co-exist peacefully, no longer as
white masters, enjoying wealth and privilege while the
locals serve us.

I abhor violence. How could I not, after what I have lived

through? The conditions for the workers at Bella Vista are good, better than any on the island. Reggie is in the process of buying the estate from Evie, but I have a nagging fear that our tenure here may be short-lived. I hate the thought that one day we may be forced to leave, to give up the life we both love, to abandon our home and find another. Yet whatever happens, we will get through it. Together.

Who can possibly know what the future might hold? Whatever it brings to our door, I believe Reggie and I have the strength to cope with it after what we have each gone though. And we will stay in Penang, please God.

After all the sorrow in my life, I never expected to find happiness. I thought I was blighted. Cursed even. The woman with two dead fiancés. A damaged survivor of the Sumatran camps. How wrong I was.

Each morning, as the sunlight slips through the slats of the wooden shutters and I feel a soft breeze on my face, I am filled with contentment. In the evenings, sitting with Reggie on the veranda sipping a sundowner, I listen to the sound of the cicadas and together we watch the fireflies dancing towards us in the dark and I tell myself I am blessed. What happened to me in the war has made me see the world with a different perspective. It has made me notice and be thankful for small things.

Sometimes, I prepare a picnic and we take Frances and climb up to a little plateau at the top of the estate. Up there we can see the straits and the distant peak of Kedah on the mainland. The birdsong is magical, and it feels like we three are the only people in this place of paradise.

On the anniversary of Frank's death in December, Reggie and I took the ferry across the strait to Butterworth, to drop flowers over the side into the waters that are his grave. We will do this every year as long as we are able, as long as we are here in Penang. There is no official memorial for the RAF and Australian Airforce men who died here – just as there is no official graveyard or headstone for my mother and Veronica and all the others who died in those vile camps in Sumatra. They all live on in my memories.

As we stand side-by-side, watching our garland of flowers drift across the calm waters of the straits, I reach for Reggie's hand and he squeezes mine in return.

THE END

To learn more about Mary and for Evie's story, read the best-selling *The Pearl of Penang*, the novel that precedes *Prisoner from Penang*. "*This book hit me in the gut. It was magical to read and will stay with me for some time. Wonderful.*"

Find out more about *The Pearl of Penang* on Clare's website

https://clareflynn.co.uk/the-pearl-of-penang.html

Newsletter

To sign up for Clare's monthly newsletter and the chance for great offers, competitions and more go to https://www.subscribepage.com/r4wiu5 – as a special thank you there's an exclusive gift of Clare's short story collection, *A Fine Pair of Shoes and Other Stories.*

IF YOU ENJOYED PRISONER FROM PENANG

It would be fantastic if you could spare a few minutes to leave a review at the retailer where you bought the book.

Reviews make a massive difference to authors - they help books get discovered by other readers and make it easier for authors to get promotional support – some promotions require a minimum number of reviews in order for a book to be accepted. Your words can make a difference.

Thank you!

CLARE'S NEWSLETTER

Why not subscribe to Clare's monthly newsletter? Clare will update you on her work in progress, her travels, and you'll be the first to know when she does a cover reveal, shares an extract, or has news of special offers and promotions. She often asks for input from her subscribers on cover design, book titles and characters' names.

Don't worry - your email address will NEVER be shared with a third party and if you reply to any of the newsletters you will get a personal response from Clare. She LOVES hearing from readers.

As a special thank you, you'll get a free download of her short story collection, *A Fine Pair of Shoes and Other Stories*

Here's the link to sign up - Click below or go to clareflynn.co.uk to the sign-up form. (Privacy Policy on Clare's website)

https://www.subscribepage.com/r4wIu5

ACKNOWLEDGMENTS

I am indebted in particular to two accounts of the experiences of women imprisoned by the Japanese during the Second World War.

The Real Tenko by Mark Felton examines prisoner experiences across the whole Pacific theatre while *Women Beyond the Wire* by Lavinia Warner and John Sandilands focuses on the Sumatran camps. The latter was the background to the stories and characters in the 1970s British television series *Tenko* and the more recent feature film *Paradise Road*. These books, as well as other biographical accounts, demonstrate the conditions under which the women and children existed in the prison camps and were invaluable sources. I chose not to watch the two fictionalised accounts, as I wanted to be free to shape my own story and characters without influence. The central story of Mary's captivity is the product of my imagination but consistent with history. Many details about everyday camp life are drawn from the true accounts.

I have included references to actual events, such as the

slaughter of nurses and wounded men shipwrecked from the *Vyner Brooke,* the execution of patients and medical staff in the British Military Hospital in Singapore, and the death of the airman at Muntok camp after the make-shift amputation of both his feet. Other incidents, such as the repairing of the thatched roof by a plucky Dutch nun and the terrible circumstances of the long trip between Banka and the rubber estate in Sumatra are closely based on actual events.

I borrowed heavily from history to locate the story – following the movement of the captured women between Muntok camp, the Dutch Houses at Irenelaan in Palembang, the Palembang men's camp, Muntok Atap camp in Banka and finally the isolated Dutch rubber plantation at Belalu.

The evacuation of Singapore was indeed botched and the Japanese navy and airforce bombed and shipwrecked several vessels carrying women and children – the *Kuala* lost off PomPong island in particular.

The diet, diseases, daily routines and treatment of the women in the camps draws directly on real experiences and the composition of the camps by nationality is consistent with the facts.

My characters may have experienced some of the tribulations the real women went through, but are entirely fictitious, so too are the Japanese guards, including Shoei.

As always, thanks to my wonderful editor, Debi Alper, designer Jane Dixon-Smith, and Eastbourne critique group partners, Margaret, jay, Maureen and Joanna. A big thanks to my fabulous eagle-eyed readers Debbie Marmor, JT Carey, Jill Hiatt, Lynn Osborne, Cyndi Wannamaker and Irene, who all kindly did a pre-publication proof-read on super-fast timing. To the Facebook Second World War

Authors group, particularly Marion Kummerow, who provided the impetus to write this book. To my wonderful author friends in 'The Sanctuary' who are a constant source of advice, encouragement and empathy. Most of all, to my loyal readers who make this possible and so worthwhile.

ABOUT THE AUTHOR

Clare Flynn is the author of eleven historical novels and a collection of short stories. She is the winner of the Book-Brunch 2020 Selfies Award for Adult Fiction. A former Marketing Director and strategy consultant, she was born in Liverpool and has lived in London, Newcastle, Paris, Milan, Brussels and Sydney and is now enjoying being in Eastbourne on the Sussex coast where she can see the sea and the Downs from her windows.

When not writing, she loves to travel (often for research purposes) and enjoys painting in oils and watercolours as well as making patchwork quilts and learning to play the piano again.

Read more about Clare and her books on her website https://clareflynn.co.uk

READ THE FIRST CHAPTER OF THE PEARL OF PENANG

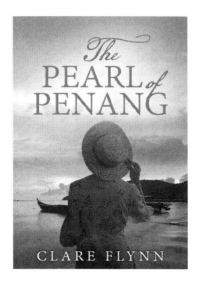

1
_____

When the letter from Douglas Barrington arrived, Evie Fraser was at breakfast. Instead of eating, she was thumbing through the situations vacant pages of *The Lady* magazine. It was a weekly ritual that Mrs Shipley-Thomas, her elderly employer, had long since given up complaining about. After nine years working as a paid companion, Evie would have loved to break free and try something different. But every time she identified a position that might be promising, she weighed it against her current one and found it wanting or insufficiently different to justify the upheaval and the inevitable distress of her employer. Mrs Shipley-Thomas was all too aware of Evie's frustrations, but had grown complacent, believing her companion would never do anything about them.

A letter addressed to Evie was a rare occurrence. Mrs Shipley-Thomas looked up from shuffling through her own correspondence and frowned. 'This one's for you, my dear. It looks rather interesting. All the way from Malaya. Judging by the number of times it's been forwarded, it's a wonder it got here at all.' She tapped the envelope with a fingernail.

'I don't know anyone in Malaya.' Evie put down her teacup.

'It seems you do, my dear. Perhaps it's a long-lost admirer trying to track you down. Not that it's any of my business.' The old lady snorted, evidently amused at the improbability of her paid companion having such a thing as a gentleman friend.

Evie reached to take the missive, feeling a little frisson of excitement, then braced herself for disappointment. Nothing in her life ever justified a sense of anticipation. She turned the envelope over in her hands. It had been forwarded from her former home to her family's solicitors and thence to here.

Unfolding the thin paper, she flattened out the crease. It was written using a typewriter and its sender must have positioned the paper in the carriage at an angle so the words were sloping slightly from left to right, probably unintentionally. The keys had been hit so hard that in places the letters had pierced the paper. It indicated haste and a lack of care, probably executed by someone unaccustomed to typing. The date was about seven weeks earlier. She glanced at the bottom of the page first and saw it was from her mother's cousin, Douglas Barrington.

Penang
February 15th 1939

Dear Evelyn,
News of the death of your father has finally reached me here. Please accept my belated condolences. I also understand your mother is now living in America and that you are unattached.

I will come straight to the point. Following the death of my wife, Felicity, I am in need of support and companionship and it occurred to me that our interests may coincide. If you are willing, I am prepared to make you an offer of marriage. I regret that the distance involved and my business commitments here in Malaya prevent my journeying to England to ask you in person.

If this offer is acceptable to you, I will make arrangements for your passage to Penang. My friend, Arthur Leighton, the District Officer here, will be in England on home leave with his wife Veronica, returning in late June and they have offered to accompany you on the voyage. I look forward to hearing your response. If I have misunderstood your circumstances, please accept my apologies.

Yours sincerely
Douglas Barrington

'OH, MY GOODNESS!' Evie dropped the letter, then picked it up and read it again. 'How extraordinary!'

'Don't keep me in suspense, dear girl. Spill the beans.'

'It's a proposal of marriage.'

'By letter? Gracious! These modern men. Who on earth is it from?'

'You'd better read it.' Evie held out the piece of paper.

'I don't have my glasses. Just give me the gist.'

'It's from my mother's cousin. He's asked me to travel to Malaya and marry him.'

'Heavens above. Your mother's cousin? He must be far too old for you.' She picked up the sugar tongs and dropped a lump into her tea.

'Actually, he's younger than Mummy. About twelve years older than me.'

And have you met this ill-mannered man?'

'Just once. At his wedding. I was only fifteen. He danced with me.' She closed her eyes, summoning up the memory. What she didn't say was that it had been the most thrilling thing that had ever happened to her. He had been the most handsome man she'd ever seen. Thinking about it now made her feel giddy with the romance of that moment.

'At his wedding?' Mrs Shipley-Thomas looked horrified.

'His wife has since died.'

'When?'

'He doesn't say.'

'And based on one dance with you many moons ago he's decided you'll make him a suitable spouse?' She gave a little snort. 'You must have made a big impression.'

'I'm surprised he remembers me at all. He appears to have made the offer on the assumption that I'm on the shelf and desperate.'

'Well you are, aren't you?' Mrs Shipley-Thomas gave another little snort. 'How old are you now, Evelyn? Thirty?'

'Twenty-seven.'

'I think that qualifies you as an old maid.'

Evie pushed back her chair, sending her tea sloshing into the saucer.

'Do be careful, dear. You really are the clumsiest girl. Where are you going now?'

'To write my reply.'

'Good show. Waste no time in sending him packing.'

'I mean to say yes.'

'What?' Mrs Shipley-Thomas's face contorted with shock.

'I intend to accept his proposal. You're quite right. I *am* desperate to avoid becoming an old maid. And I can think of nothing more exciting than going to live in a faraway place and marry a handsome man.'

'You're not serious. You can't possibly do that. I was only teasing you about being an old maid. I didn't mean it. Don't be hasty. At least give it some thought. Malaya is a long way away.' She gripped the edge of the table, the blood draining from her face. 'Besides – what will become of me?'

'You've plenty of time to find another paid companion. I won't be leaving until the end of June. Mr Barrington has to make the travel arrangements.' Evie picked up her copy of *The Lady* and handed it across the table. 'There are plenty of promising candidates advertising their services in here.'

Heart hammering, she left the room, her dignity only slightly impacted by tripping and stumbling on the rug.

Safely in her bedroom, Evie leaned against the closed door, waiting for her pulse to stop racing and her chest heaving. What had she done? It wasn't too late to go back downstairs and tell Mrs Shipley-Thomas she'd had second thoughts. Her employer would be relieved and Evie could remain in her safe cosy world where nothing out of the ordinary ever happened. A short business-like letter to Douglas Barrington and the episode would be forgotten and her life could go on as before.

She moved over to her desk and took up a piece of writing paper and her fountain pen.

Dear Douglas

Thank you for your kind thoughts regarding the loss of my father. His death was a great shock but I have had nearly nine years to adjust to life without him and my mother.

Thank you also for your offer of marriage. I regret I am unable to accept

Evie struggled to come up with an acceptable basis to refuse her cousin's proposal. She could hardly write *because I am scared stiff,* yet in truth that was the only reason for her reticence.

The death of her father, his decision to take his own life rather than face the consequences when he was caught up in a financial scandal, had knocked Evie for six. Even now, years later, she missed him and despite what he had done, grieved for him and felt abandoned. When her mother had wasted no time after his death before joining her long-term lover in the United States, Evie's world contracted further. While she and her mother had always had a strained and distant relationship, finding herself completely alone had not been easy. Her dreams of marrying, or of pursuing her education, were shattered. Becoming a lady's companion had been based on necessity not inclination.

Hands propped under her chin, she tried to think it through. It was foolish to let annoyance at Mrs Shipley-Thomas's insensitivity push her into a decision with lifelong consequences. Something so momentous required a more measured and rational approach. She must set aside her emotions and let her head rule her. Taking another piece of paper, she drew a line down the centre and headed one column *Reasons to Accept* and the other, *Reasons to Refuse*, and began to fill in the spaces beneath.

The arguments for refusing consisted of:

I barely know him

I have no idea what living in Malaya would be like

He's much older than me

His letter was blunt with no hint of romance

Once I go I may not be able to come back

It's a huge risk

After a few minutes she crossed out the third item. Twelve years wasn't that much of an age gap and hardly a reason in itself not to marry Douglas Barrington. She drew a circle around the last item, as that was the crux of the matter – the other points were all different aspects of risk.

Turning to the empty first column she wrote:

Dancing with Douglas Barrington was one of the most exciting and memorable moments of my life

I've always wanted something interesting to happen to me

I hate living here

I'm bored with working for Mrs ST

Mrs ST doesn't appreciate me

If I don't do this I'll spend the rest of my life wondering what might have happened

This is probably my last and only chance for love, marriage and a family

Douglas is the most handsome man I've ever met.

She read the list again and thought it sounded very childish and superficial. She crossed out the last point. On reflection the most salient point was the one about spending the rest of her life wondering 'what if?'. She drew a circle round that. In the end it all boiled down to whether she wanted to grasp hold of life or cower timorously and carry on with her humdrum existence.

She dipped her pen in the inkwell and filled it. Taking a new sheet of paper, she crafted her reply to Douglas Barrington.

A TELEGRAM ARRIVED from Douglas Barrington two weeks later, advising Evie that his friend, Arthur Leighton would be in touch about travel arrangements. Mrs Shipley-Thomas pleaded with Evie to stay, offering her first a bigger bedroom with a view over the garden, then when that failed, a substantial pay rise. Evie was determined to resist such blandishments, telling herself that if her employer valued her so highly she should have offered them before there was the threat of her leaving. When the pleading became anger and resentful silences, Evie knew she had made the right choice. Mrs Shipley-Thomas was governed entirely by self-interest and clearly didn't give a fig about Evie's welfare and future. After all, why should she? As the weeks passed, Evie's fears diminished and her excitement grew. She couldn't wait to get on the ship and wave goodbye to dreary England and her dreary life.

As soon as a suitable replacement was found within the pages of *The Lady*, Mrs Shipley-Thomas told Evie she would pay her wages until the agreed leaving date, but she would like her to go now, as Miss Prendergast, the new companion, was willing to start immediately. Relieved to be free of what had become an oppressive atmosphere, Evie took a room in a boarding house in a cheap and unfashionable area of London while she waited for the date she was due to sail.

Mr Leighton had been in touch by letter to suggest Evie meet his wife for lunch, in order that Veronica might impart some advice about life in Malaya and what Evie needed to pack for the journey.

The women arranged to meet in the restaurant in Marshall and Snelgrove. Anxious to make a good impression, Evie wore her best suit, even though it was too warm that day for wool and it was a little dated. In her haste, she got on the Tube in the wrong direction and had travelled four stops before she realised her mistake. Late for the appointment, she had to miss her planned visit to the powder room to repair her lipstick and check that her slip wasn't showing. As a result she was hot and dishevelled when she rushed into the restaurant, before remembering that she had no idea what Veronica Leighton looked like.

Standing on the threshold, Evie looked about, trying to decide which of the unaccompanied women might be the wife of a senior civil servant. She approached a matronly woman in her late forties, but it wasn't her. About to enquire of a harassed mother with a baby – Mrs Leighton may well have a child – she felt a tap on her shoulder and almost jumped out of her skin.

'Miss Fraser?'

Spinning round, she nearly crashed into the speaker, who took a step backwards. 'Steady on!' the woman said curtly.

'So sorry. You're Mrs Leighton?'

Slender and willowy, Mrs Leighton had the grace and figure of a ballet dancer. Her dark glossy hair was swept back into a tight chignon. Big almond-shaped eyes were highlighted with kohl and mascara, and her pale skin had a translucent glow that belied the fact she lived in a hot climate. Her mouth was a tight Cupid's bow, glossy with the brightest, reddest lipstick Evie had ever seen. She was dressed in a deep green silk costume that looked as if it came from Paris, set off by a pearl necklace that left no doubt as to its authenticity. Automatically, Evie put up a hand to cover her own cultured pearls, then dropped it. There was no point. She knew she must appear cheap and shabby next to this exotic and expensively-dressed goddess.

Mrs Leighton looked Evie up and down critically – Evie detected a slight curl of the lip. Perspiration beaded on Evie's forehead. Damn the silly choice of a woollen suit when it was early summer.

'I'm frightfully sorry I'm late. I got on the wrong underground line.'

Mrs Leighton's eyebrows lifted. 'Always better to take a cab, darling,' she drawled. 'The underground's so grubby.'

Evie felt shabby and awkward. In contrast, Mrs Leighton was like a rare butterfly.

With the slightest inclination of her carefully coiffed

head, Mrs Leighton summoned the head waiter to show them to their table. It was a corner one with a good view of the room, yet a distance away from the mêlée. 'Thank you, Robert,' she said, breathily, conveying in her intimate tone that she was a familiar and much-valued guest.

Once they were seated, Evie said, 'You're a regular here, Mrs Leighton?'

'What makes you think that?'

'You seem to know the waiter.'

Mrs Leighton gave a little laugh. 'I make it my business to behave as though every waiter is my dear friend. That way one gets the best table and the best service.'

'But you knew his name.'

'Only because I asked him. Really, darling, don't you do the same?'

'To be honest I never eat in restaurants.'

Mrs Leighton made no verbal response, but Evie sensed disdain mixed with amusement. She squirmed inside, her palms clammy. This was going to be an ordeal.

They made their choices from the menu – for Evie, lamb cutlets, for her companion, a salad. No wonder she was so svelte.

Veronica Leighton leaned forward, her gaze fierce. 'How long have you known Dougie?'

Evie stammered. 'He's my mother's only cousin. So I suppose all my life.'

'That's not what I meant. How *well* do you know him?'

Blood rushed to Evie's cheeks. 'Not well at all.' She hesitated then, unable to dissimulate under the gaze of Mrs Leighton, added, 'We've actually only met once. At his wedding. Years ago.' About to add that they had danced together, she stopped herself in time.

'Poor dear Felicity. Dougie was devoted to her. He was utterly devastated when she died. We all were.'

Evie fidgeted with her napkin. 'I remember she was very beautiful.'

'As an angel. Graceful,' she said pointedly. 'And a wonderful person too. So full of life. Always smiling and laughing. Such fun. Everyone adored Felicity.'

'How did she die?'

'You don't know?' Mrs Leighton frowned as Evie shook her head. 'Malaria. Three years ago. Tragic. So terribly, terribly sad.'

The waiter brought their food, but Mrs Leighton barely paused. Her salad lay untouched as she continued to speak. Evie tucked guiltily into her cutlets but pushed the potatoes aside.

'Of course, none of us expected Dougie to marry again. We're all utterly mystified.' Her piercing eyes fixed on Evie and she gave a little shake of her head, which conveyed that the mystery was even greater now that she'd actually met the intended bride. Evie wanted to get up and run out of the room but she made herself sit it out.

Mrs Leighton answered her own question. 'I imagine it's because he needs a son. The one thing dear Felicity didn't give him. Just little Jasmine. And he can't possibly hand his inheritance on to her.'

'Jasmine? He has a daughter?' Evie put down her knife and fork, appetite gone.

'Gracious! You don't know Dougie at all, do you? Jasmine is seven years old and is living in a convent on the mainland.'

'The mainland?'

The tutting was barely disguised. 'Penang is an island. Haven't you even looked at a map, Miss Fraser?'

Evie, mortified, couldn't manage another mouthful. Mrs Leighton made her feel like a naughty schoolgirl – one lacking in any sophistication and by implication clearly an unsuitable spouse for Douglas Barrington. Her face must be red and blotchy and she wished she'd had time to stop at the powder room.

Drawing air deep into her lungs she let it out slowly. 'Mrs Leighton,' she said at last. 'As you will have gathered, I know next to nothing of Douglas Barrington and his current circumstances. After my father died, my mother went to live in America and I'm afraid I lost track of family matters.'

Mrs Leighton pushed her untouched salad away and motioned for the waiter to remove it. 'So, what on earth possessed you to accept a marriage proposal from a man you hardly know?'

'If you don't mind me saying, Mrs Leighton, I'd prefer not to answer that. Your husband suggested that you might be willing to offer me some advice about living in Malaya. What kind of clothing I need to bring. That sort of thing. If you're not prepared to do that, I will pay the bill and bid you goodbye. I have a lot to do before we sail.'

Leaning back in her chair, Mrs Leighton nodded. 'So you *can* stand up for yourself. That's good. You'll need to with Dougie. I was worried you were going to be a doormat. Believe me, he'll try to make you one.' She glanced around the room and caught the eye of their waiter. 'Why don't I order us each a "Gin and It"? We can have a good chat and then look at clothes together. Cotton and linen. Just day dresses – you can buy silk over there and get your evening gowns made up. There's a fabulous little Indian chappie who can run up a gown in an afternoon. I'll introduce you. He can copy a design straight out of *Vogue*. For daywear keeping cool is the thing. It's hot as blazes in Penang. All year round. You can probably get rid of most of your wardrobe as it's far too steamy for things like that.' She gestured dismissively at Evie's wool suit.

Clapping her hands together she said, 'How does that sound? Oh, and shall we dispense with the formalities? Call me Veronica.' Her mouth formed a smile that her eyes didn't echo.

At least the full-on attack had stopped, but Evie had already decided that Mrs Veronica Leighton was a first-class bitch.

Half an hour later, having written a list dictated by Mrs Leighton of essential items to bring with her to Penang, Evie had had enough advice and was determined it wasn't going to extend to choosing her new wardrobe. Quite apart from being bossed around, the kind of clothes Mrs Leighton had in mind would be beyond her limited budget. Pleading a headache, she made her escape and took the much-maligned underground to High Street Kensington and bought herself a couple of cheap cotton frocks and some new underwear in Barkers. She could get more clothes made when she got to Malaya. Her existing wardrobe was unsuitable for a hot climate. At the suggestion of the land-lady of her boarding house, she took her winter clothing to a nearby church, for distribution to the poor. Her limited funds were now almost exhausted. She'd need to stretch the pennies until the sailing date in a week's time.

That night, as she lay in bed, struggling to sleep, she wondered whether she'd made a terrible mistake in agreeing to marry Douglas Barrington. One thing she had not included on her decision-making list was the question of why Douglas had made such an offer in the first place. It now seemed reckless of him – and even more reckless of her in accepting.

Why on earth had he asked her to marry him? And why hadn't he mentioned he had a daughter? Would the little girl be living with them after they were married? Was he really only marrying her to father a son? Why choose her? He barely knew her.

Veronica's words kept repeating in her head. How could Evie ever expect to replace the beautiful Felicity? She'd been crazy to think she might. And hadn't Veronica said that all Douglas's friends were amazed at his decision – and all of them had adored Felicity?

Tossing and turning on the lumpy mattress, she thought back to the wedding of twelve years ago. The bride had been breathtakingly beautiful and a perfect match for her dashing groom. While Douglas Barrington had indeed danced with the teenage Evie, he'd also danced with almost every woman present that day. She was deluded to imagine that he had retained the memory of her over the years. But she couldn't help hoping that he had, that he might even one day come to care for her. Then reality struck again. How could she, a woman more at home on a hockey pitch than a dance floor, ever hope to win the love and affection of such a man?

A WEEK LATER, Evie stood on the quayside looking around, trying to spot the Leightons among the crowd thronging the waterfront. She couldn't board the ship yet as Mr Leighton was to meet her and hand over her ticket. Most of the people on the dock appeared to be friends and relatives there to wave off passengers. She began to panic.

'Yoo hoo! Evelyn!' The call came from above.

Looking up, Evie saw Veronica Leighton leaning over the guard rail on one of the upper decks of the ship, waving a silk scarf as though she were a French revolutionary leading the mob into battle.

A man appeared beside Evie, his hand extended in greeting. 'You must be Evelyn. I'm Arthur Leighton. Pleased to meet you.'

Evie had to hide her surprise at Veronica's husband. Her assumption had been that scary Veronica would be married to a handsome lounge lizard. But instead of a suave and elegant roué, Arthur Leighton looked more like a school-master: dishevelled, with a thick mop of sandy hair that flopped over his brow until he brushed it away with his fingers. He appeared to be younger than his wife, but Evie had never been good at guessing people's ages. With one finger he pushed up his spectacles from where they had slipped down his nose, and grinned at her with a wide and genuine smile. Arthur Leighton reminded her of a Labrador puppy and Evie knew at once she was going to like him.

ALSO BY CLARE FLYNN

The Pearl of Penang

Kurinji Flowers

Letters from a Patchwork Quilt

The Green Ribbons

The Gamekeeper's Wife

A Greater World

Storms Gather Between Us

The Canadians collection

The Chalky Sea

The Alien Corn

The Frozen River

Printed in Great Britain
by Amazon